Wild Hearts Elephant Sanctuary Book 1

THEY CALLED ME JANE

APRIL O'CONNELL

ISBN: 978-1-945169-26-7

Orison Publishers, Inc.
PO Box 188
Grantham, PA 17027
717-731-1405
www.OrisonPublishers.com
Publish your book now, marsha@orisonpublishers.com

Printed in the United States of America

For

Logan and Jaden

"Always follow your dreams,
no matter where they take you.
I love you."

~MomMom

Acknowledgements

I would like to thank my daughter, Amber, and my son-in-law, Aaron, for their constant support and excitement for my writing.

To my sisters, Shannon, Jo, and Heidi, thank you for reading and giving honest feedback. To all of my friends, and you know who you are, thank you for your insights and suggestions as well.

To Laura Swarr, owner of Vintage Bloom Photography, you have an amazing talent and passion for your art. Your photography is an inspiration to me. You made Zura come to life in my mind.

Many thanks to Teri Miller for your editing skills, encouragement, and passion for my story.

Table of Contents

PROLOGUE

The gun went off and I felt a stab of heat in my thigh that toppled me. I knew if I succumbed to the pain, I wouldn't stand a chance of getting out of this alive. I could hear Cha-Cha growling on the ridge, but I couldn't see him and I was sure he couldn't see me. I knew if I called out, I'd give away my position on the ledge. The water below churned violently. I didn't have much time to make a decision. I had to either go back up the cliff or find a way down. And I had to do it before Bain made it to the top."

CHAPTER 1

August 1920

There was something magical about the jungle just after dawn. The night's carnage was over, and those who were lucky to survive the onslaught of predators lived to see another day.

Although there was no perfect time to travel in the jungle, daybreak usually felt the safest. My reasoning was the predator's stomachs were full, so I might not look like their next tasty meal. And I used the trees for my passage. It was safer than being on the ground.

Each day's travels took me to familiar sites. But I wanted more. I pushed just a little beyond the areas I'd covered the previous day and pressed my imaginary circle farther into the jungle's trees. The larger my circle grew, the more confident I became.

It was a race for me every day to see if I could be out of bed and dressed and outside to witness the dawn.

I liked to feel the heat from the sun's rising on my face. The rays made me feel happy to be touched by its newly risen day.

Last year, when I was ten-years-old, still very young in most people's eyes, I began the exploring. I found excuses and ways to disappear. My mother hated it—when she was attentive enough to notice, which didn't happen often. She had an obsession with charting and studying the elephants that lived at the Wild Hearts Elephant Sanctuary and the herd that visited the field beyond our land. It consumed her days, her thoughts, her actions.

Before I turned ten, Momma made me go with her to the field and sit there while she worked. I would interrupt her all the time. I would ask her questions about what she was doing, why she was doing it, and any random question that came to my mind so that she would tell me to go and play.

It wasn't until I turned ten that I begged her not to make me go with her. I promised to be good, to do my chores, and to stay out of trouble. That, of course, was sort of a half-truth. Oh, I did my chores. I tried to be good. And for the most part, I stayed out of trouble. But trouble seemed to find me. I was forever coming home with cuts and scrapes. Several times I needed stitches, which upset my father. I would argue that none of the situations were my fault. It was purely from the circumstances of growing up in a jungle. Things were bound to happen. Accidents were just one slide on a slippery rock away, one sting from an insect, or even a slight fall from a tree. It wasn't that I was clumsy. I was just very active. And I was curious. My father used to say that curiosity killed the cat. I knew he meant that being curious led to me getting into trouble. That may have been true, but I didn't go searching for trouble, it just sort of found me.

At age eleven, I knew I had to split my time between working on my swing in the trees and helping to care for the animals. Big or small, they required the same level of care and attention.

Baby elephants needed lots of love and food. And they'd leave giant messes that required someone to clean it up. I must admit that while I do love the elephants and consider them my brothers and sisters, I never get excited about cleaning up their dung. Who would?

I compromised with myself. I did my chores very early in the morning without complaining and then I would be free to play. I had a great big jungle in front of me, and I wanted to explore it all.

When I completed the day's chores, I would race toward the trees—discovering and climbing, swinging up high. I knew which branches would hold my weight, and which could potentially result in my untimely death. I would count the number of seconds it would take me to reach a particularly large tree at the densest part of my imaginary circle in the jungle. It helped me to see whether my climbing skills were improving. Most days they were.

Sneaking away from the sanctuary was easy. The hard part was trying to determine where I would explore next. Would it be the trees with the monkeys or the cave behind the waterfall? Sometimes I would just start walking and figure it out once I got past all the watchful eyes at home.

My parents created the Wild Hearts Elephant Sanctuary. Board by board, they built our home, a large barn, and an office attached to the animal hospital for my father to tend to the injured elephants. "It was a labor of love," Momma would say.

The success of Wild Hearts Elephant Sanctuary was my parents' passion, and they worked tirelessly securing funds to care for the orphaned and injured elephants. It often took my father away from us, but it was necessary to keep the funds coming into the sanctuary.

My father always insisted on being part of the rescue to transport the newly orphaned elephants to our sanctuary for care. Being a veterinarian, Father would manage to use a tranquilizer if he needed to, to keep the animal from hurting itself or anyone else.

He and the team would sometimes leave for a few days, which left my mother and me alone to tend to all the chores.

Hearing my father's truck pulling out, I would listen for sounds of my mother. She always said the same thing just before she left for the day.

"Zura, I am going to work," she would call. "Stay close to the house and stay out of trouble."

"Have a good day!" I always responded without making any promises to either of her requests.

When I heard the sound of Momma's voice humming her favorite song and the screen door slam, I knew it was time to move.

I would go out the back door and sneak around behind the animal hospital, passing the barn where the new arrival of elephants were kept, and I would disappear out of sight.

I was free to venture where most girls my age would probably fear to go.

Now and then, something would trip me up. Like the time a black mamba was on my path. I had to adjust my steps to avoid that nasty deadly snake. Or the time when a troop of mandrills decided that I was too close to them. Those monkeys could intimidate anyone with their light blue faces, those red noses, and those terrifying teeth. The males began to show aggression toward me by baring those incredibly long fangs and beating the ground furiously. I knew them to be omnivores; they would eat anything. Since I was only ten at the time and about the size of a springbok antelope, I didn't want to risk being a meal and got out of their way quickly. I was lucky that they didn't catch up to me. They probably would have killed me—or at least tried.

Several weeks after my eleventh birthday, I found a beautiful waterfall surrounded by trees and wildlife and a fantastic and dangerous-looking cliff. Because I feared almost nothing—yet—I decided to figure out the best way to scale the cliff. It took me a whole month to figure out exactly where to put my feet. With each try, I got closer and closer to the top. When I felt that I could go no further, or I was feeling intimidated by the height, I would climb back down.

I named the cliff Thinking Rock because I had to use my brain to figure out just how to climb it.

I visited Thinking Rock every chance I got, trying to find new ways to reach its peak. Sadly, one time I fell when I was only a short distance from the bottom and twisted my ankle pretty bad. My mother was furious with what she called my careless ways.

I was sure Thinking Rock was known by another name in some book somewhere, but it's also where I would go to think and dream.

On the day I reached the peak, I felt like I could accomplish anything. I was the princess of the jungle. It felt like I was standing on the top of the world, looking out at the jungle valley below.

The cliff's solid rocks jetted out in different lengths. Ledges looked even more menacing when I stood on the edge and peered over the side. The treetops were magnificent, like a soft cloud of green blanketing the earth below.

I could see the waterfall and its magnificent power rushing toward the river beneath, pounding the rocks and making rainbows with the help of the rays coming from the sun. Though the waterfall was not as high as the cliff, the view was impressive. It too had its secrets. Like a hidden cave behind the raging waters.

And like those secrets, there were things hidden I had yet to encounter which would change my life forever.

I will never forget that one day that started just like any other, but ended in a way I would never have imagined.

The field behind our house was empty of animals, so I felt safe to sprint to the tree line.

As I was climbing up one of my favorite cape fig tree, I imagined sitting in a field, surrounded by nature's goodness and pretending that I was the jungle's special princess. How I longed for lace dresses and beautiful curls. But I couldn't dream for too long and forget about my surroundings. I returned to the present to take notice at first that the animals were on high alert.

The monkey's screeched their warning calls. There was a scurry of smaller animals on the jungle floor.

It usually meant that a bigger, more dangerous animal was moving through the jungle.

Not on this day. I could smell them before I could see them. The strangers smelled of man sweat and cigars. Not the kind of cigars that my father would smoke on occasion. These were strong and peppery. The smoke made my mouth go dry. The odor that the men actually gave off was overpowering to my sensitive nose.

The next thing that I noticed was how well I could hear them. They must have alerted every species within a three-mile radius that they were in the jungle. Heavy steps and loud voices boomed in the air.

I was curious and decided to follow them from the safety of the canopy. Creeping silently through the rooftop of the trees, I moved stealthily. I pretended they were prey and I was stalking their every move. Their movements were slow, like a snail. It allowed me to take my time and calculate the best routes to take.

It was amusing to pretend that I was a hunter and hungry for my next kill. I tracked them as I let my imagination run away with me. Becoming the mighty lioness, stalking the next meal for my family. I crouched and effortlessly glided to safety in the next tree.

I knew the jungle like the back of my hand, and I used it to my advantage.

They noisily cleared a path through the vegetation, and as soon as they passed the area, the bush swallowed up their tracks. It was as if the jungle was offended by their presence and erased all signs of their invasion.

The line of ten men stopped for a break and I halted the pretend attack. I crouched low into the leaves and watched with my keen eyes.

Three men who looked to be native to Africa were carrying the bulk of the gear. One of the natives who was leading the caravan spoke Swahili to the others as he guided them on their journey.

Four men belonged, and I guessed that the others were from far away because they apparently didn't understand the importance of jungle safety.

The foreigners looked as though they were not accustomed to the heat. They drank excessively from canteens, and mopped at their sweat with white cloths before returning them to their shirt pockets. The men swatted at bugs and backed away from entirely harmless creatures, while getting too close to the ones that could kill them.

I wanted to get a closer look at the group, so I climbed down below the tops of the trees. Still hidden well, I doubted that the loud group would ever notice me. The hefty white man, who looked to be about sixty with his gray hair showing from under his hat, was barking out orders. He was dressed in all tan as many did on safaris to blend in with the surroundings. I guessed he was the leader when everyone seemed to obey his every command.

There was a young boy with the group who stayed close to the large man. He looked to be a little older than me, but not too much. He had brownish hair like mine and was tall and thin. He had the same eyes as the enormous older man. I guessed that they were relatives. The boy seemed to stay as close as he could to the man without running into the back of him with his sudden stops.

Fear danced across the boy's face. His eyes widened as he looked in every direction. He was out of his element and looking as if he would jump out of his skin at the sight of danger. The boy was an easy target for any predator looking for an easy meal. I almost pitied him. Almost.

The movements of the tall man were hard to miss. He had a frightening face. His disfigured appearance looked as though he had been in a fight with a huge animal and he lost the battle. The shape of the deep purple scratches reminded me of the lion's powerful claws and the damage they could inflict. There was no blood that I could tell from my height, but the gashes were memorable. His khaki shorts had stains of either a dark liquid or maybe blood. The man's sweat-stained and tattered button-down white shirt had seen better days. He wore boots that looked old and weathered and a pith helmet, which was customary on a safari trip. His rifle was enormous—bigger than any that we had at the sanctuary. He effortlessly flung it over his shoulder and wore it with ease, as if it were always a part of his wardrobe. The hair on the back of my neck rose when I looked at him. A gut feeling told me everything about him was dangerous.

The African men continuously spoke to each other in Swahili. Because I spoke English and Swahili just as effortlessly, I understood them, as well as the foreigners. The African men were talking about the trip not being worth the money they were paid. They complained that the fat man and the two older men were keeping them from getting to their destination. They called them *ajizi*, which means lazy.

The further the group traveled, the more nervous they appeared.

I climbed lower to try to catch what everyone was saying. I didn't want to miss a word of the interaction between the men. When I moved, I got careless. My foot slipped. The jarring on the branch sent the tree limb shaking. Leaves floated down to the jungle floor.

The startled boy stopped and looked up at the tree; shading his eyes with his hand, he looked right at me. I could tell that he heard something by the way he perked up. He continued to strain to try to see what had caused the movement, but I remained completely still so as not to draw attention to my location. My brown shorts and tan and green top were the perfect camouflage. And I was a master at staying still—a skill that comes in very handy in the jungle. I held my breath and remained as silent as I could, waiting for him to look away.

When the boy noticed that the group was continuing without him, he lost interest in the tree and began to hurry his footsteps to catch up with the party. I was thankful that he didn't seem to find me in my hiding place. Sometimes people can't see what's right in front of them.

The group of men continued to move forward. I had a perfect seat to watch and wonder whether any of them would be attacked by the crouching lion camouflaged just 100 yards away or the poisonous snake that slithered from its resting spot on the jungle floor, something the foreigners failed to observe. The Africans talked in hushed tones among themselves. They saw the cat beyond the tree line and noticed the quick movement of the snake, thankful it did not feel threatened enough to strike.

The guide was telling the other African men about the dangers, but not one of them tried to speak English and warn the rest of the group. I figured that maybe they were already paid and didn't care what happened to the foreigners. Perhaps they hoped to rid themselves of a few of the men, probably the slow ones. But it was more likely that they did not want to panic the foreigners. If that happened, there was no telling what they might do—or what that lion might do.

As they passed a towering anthill, the boy stopped to examine it and poked it with a stick. He was probably unaware that *Siafu*, African driver ants, are furiously protective, and though it was unlikely that they would devour a human child of that size, it may not stop them from biting. I couldn't see from my height whether or not the ants were forming in protest to his mutilation of their home, but I imagined that their army would swarm and protect what was theirs until the bitter end.

Stupid boy, I thought.

The large man coughed into his sweaty white cloth and called out.

"Boy! Keep up or we leave you behind. This is not the time to dawdle. We need to get in and get out quickly, so I'll not have you toddling behind and keeping us from what we are here to do. Now keep up!"

The boy let out a loud sigh, threw the stick into the trees and scurried ahead. Just when he was starting to become more relaxed with his environment, he was making the fat man angry. He caught up with the group without much exertion.

I effortlessly swung from branch to branch and kept up with the men.

The men from Africa seemed nervous as they moved closer to the location of the new herd of elephants that lived a few miles from my home. The herd was about half a mile directly ahead of them in the clearing. I could make out the shape of them, but not the individual elephants. I purposely stayed away from them so that I wouldn't be reminded of how much I miss Tembo.

When I was born, the elephant we called Tembo was only a few months old. His mother had been poached right after his birth, and he came to live with us when he was such a young calf. Tembo was missing a piece of his right ear. It looked like it was bitten off. I suspected lions but couldn't be sure. That ear was how I could pick him out instantly. It made him look unique.

As I grew, so did our relationship. We played together every day. When my parents allowed it, and when it was safe, they would take Tembo and me to the river before the sun would set. He would float in the water, and I would lay on his back. We would drift as one. Those memories were precious to me.

I was completely comfortable with how fast his size tripled, while my growth was small.

Because the Swahili word for elephant is *tembo*, his name literally meant elephant.

Anytime I wanted to ride on his back, I would say, "Tembo, *chini*," and he would bend down so I could climb onto him. I would lay on him as content as if I was on the softest bed.

I rode on him all over the sanctuary, like I was a part of him. He meant safety and friendship to me. And I loved him. He was my brother. Then he was gone to live with the herd.

Elephants have incredible memories, so the hope was that they would remember him and accept him back.

My mother told me to give him his space so that he could be accepted by the herd. She thought that if he saw me, he would wander away from the others.

I reluctantly stayed away, but never forgot him, even though he probably forgot all about me.

It turned out that she was right. The elephants welcomed Tembo into their family unit and, if it was possible, seemed happy to have him back in their family, or so my mother told me from her observations.

I secretly and selfishly wanted them to reject Tembo so that we could have him back in our lives. I cried harder over losing him than ever in my life. He left, and with his departure, he stole something from me. A piece of my heart.

To be that close to Tembo again made me curious to get a glimpse of him.

I carelessly tripped on a knot in the tree, and my foot slipped, sending a shower of leaves toward the foreigners. I froze in place, afraid to be caught. I was turning out not to be the great hunter that I pretended to be.

"Filthy monkeys," the Scary-Face Man said as he raised his gun and looked through the sights. I swore that he noticed me because the gun was aimed directly at me and I held my breath. I tried to keep my legs from shaking, but the gun pointed at my chest frightened me.

He pretended to fire. "Boom," he said as he lowered the gun and continued to walk in the direction of the group of men.

I needed to be more careful and not give away my location. My scraped legs were burning from crouching for so long and from the lengthy periods that I remained still. My knees began to wobble and I decided that it was too dangerous to follow directly behind them if I didn't want to give away my presence. Instead, I went around their path, guessing that they would be entering the clearing after I reached it and I could tuck myself up high in the trees again.

There was no way I would lose them with the smell and noise they spread as easily as blood from a wound. The sound announced their presence like an enormous bull elephant crashing through the acacia trees. The animals remained on high alert and scattered out of the way as the party approached and passed. Baboons that spend most of their time on the jungle floor raced up to the high branches and began to shriek. Birds of all types took flight.

What didn't seem strange to me was the fact that the men decided to visit this part of Africa. Many people from all over the world came to Africa to see the wildlife, to feel the heartbeat of this mystic habitation, and to tour Wild Hearts—hopefully making a sizable donation to our cause.

But my instincts told me that things were not as they appeared. Nothing these men did displayed a reverence or curiosity for the nature that they trampled without a backward glance.

I had some questions about their intent. Why would they choose to travel through one of the deadliest jungles in the world to visit us, when they would have had a much better and safer trip if they would have used a truck from the town? It led me to think that these men wanted to stay hidden. But they were not going to remain hidden if they didn't stop making so much noise. Their lack of experience just made me more fascinated.

There was also the question about the men native to this country. Why would they guide them all the way around and into the jungle if they were getting paid to lead them safely to our sanctuary? The foreign men were not adapted to the mental and physical strength that it takes to travel in or near the wild.

The large man looked as if he would self-implode at any moment. He was overheated, overweight, and apparently out of his element. The only one who looked as though he could withstand the physical stamina was the Scary-Face Man.

So, who were they and why were they here?

As they reached the spot close to the clearing, the boy caught my attention. He began touching and smelling different plants. It was evident that he didn't know which plants were safe and which were deadly. It didn't stop him from feeling all of them, maybe out of boredom. He was batting at some bees with a stick and almost clipped one of the men. The man looked annoyed and swatted the boy on the back of the head with the palm of his hand.

The group came to a stop close to the field, right inside the perimeter of the trees. The Scary-Face Man raised his arm and put up a fist to motion for everyone to stop. The group obeyed their leader.

They were all busy with bags and boxes and canteens. No one was paying any attention to the trees to their left. But I was in a pretty good spot to see the elephants in the field ahead and the men below. As I regained my confidence, I silently shifted to a lower smaller branch so I could get a better look. The men carrying the gear placed it on the ground, just inside the jungle's perimeter. The hefty man who I guessed was the leader started to unpack a large, extended, leather case. He lifted a very bulky gun out of the case as another man set up a tripod to hold it.

I could finally see what they were aiming for and it sent terror into my soul. Not more than one hundred yards away was my mother's favorite herd of elephants, including Tembo. My Tembo, who was my best friend. It had been a long time since I had seen him, but there he was. He had grown. His misshaped ear warmed my heart, but I knew his beautiful tusks made him a target.

Why we sent him to live with this group of elephants and put him in danger I will never understand. To see him in harm's way was more than I could bear. His death—if it came to that—would be on our heads. My mother's head, actually, for sending him away and placing him in danger. I didn't think I could forgive her if they killed Tembo.

I climbed further out onto the branch to get a closer look. Inch by inch, I crawled on my belly and used my arms to pull me along.

A female button spider located on a smaller branch near me looked menacing. I knew to stay far away from her venomous bite. I successfully avoided the toxic spider and its sharp fangs. The spider scurried out of the way as I reached near to the end of the branch.

I watched as the large man looked through the scope on his gun and pointed in the direction of the herd. The older men were gesturing and helping to make the decision. By the nodding of their heads, I could tell that they agreed on which elephant they were going to kill.

My heart pounded out of my chest as my throat seized in fear. I tried to think quickly but I felt helpless. There was no telling what they would do to me if they discovered me in the trees. I couldn't risk discovery, so I was forced to stay silent.

The fat man raised his gun for a second time and I couldn't take my eyes off the clearing. I felt the tears of sorrow for any one of the elephants that would soon lose his or her life to the horrible men.

My stomach was in knots and my hands became sweaty. I tried to think of a way to distract the shooter from his target. I wished for lions, for gorillas, anything that would make the men run away. Nothing came.

The large man slowly directed the gun until his target was in view. He positioned the tripod and searched again for his trophy. The silence was deafening as no one moved, no one spoke, and I continued to watch the impending slaughter.

I held on tightly to the branch as it bowed under my weight and I realized that I had climbed out too far. It was too late to go back to the safety of the canopy. The limb began to crack, and I prayed that I would not fall the long distance down to my death.

As I looked back at the large man and then into the clearing, I gasped. There she was. I saw her and my soul broke. My mother stood there in the open with her book in hand above her head, waving and screaming at the man with the gun. "No! Don't!"

In a split second, with a loud boom, it was too late. My mother's arms were flailing for only a moment and then she fell, slowly crumbling to the ground. Out of instinct, I reached for her. Stretched as far as my arms would go, I reached for nothing but air. I overextended my hand, and the tears flowed. She was too far away.

Her body lay silent and still, and all of the men froze with the realization that the trophy that they wished for was not what they ended up shooting. They gasped at their horrible mistake. My beautiful mother falling to the ground was the last image that I had before I began to fall myself.

It was too late to wish for wings to fly away. There was no time to grab another branch. My descent was quick, and everything went black as the night sky.

CHAPTER 2

The poacher's shot echoed repeatedly in my head. My mother falling to the ground and lying utterly still, then me falling, helpless like a feather on the wild winds. In unison, our fates were lying in the balance. Could she heal from being shot or was she already dead? Could I manage to be in one piece after my fall, or would I die in the jungle I loved?

If I allowed myself to feel too much, I would be broken and would probably not survive. It was not the time for sadness. It was not the time to think of my mother. I had to hope that she survived. And I had to think about my fate and how to get to her.

Fury and fear consumed me and I began to shake. I hated that I was afraid. So much for the fearless girl my father thought I was. Truth be told, I was never so scared in my life. Fearful for my mother. For myself. Terrified of what the men would do with me.

Another thought crossed my mind; maybe I was already dead. It was true that I felt numb on the inside. Being killed by the fall would make sense. There was no way that I could have survived. But I did survive. And when a sudden rush of emotions came over me that only living people had to endure, I knew I was alive. I was feeling the most incredible pain in my broken heart and wanted to cry but did not dare make a sound. I never knew it was possible to feel that sort of hurt, both physically and emotionally.

Having the sense to stay completely still, I could hear the men talking in English, and I was afraid if they knew that I was active, my fate would not be good. If that happened and they killed me, I would never know the answer to that question about my mother. If the men decided they didn't want a witness and shot me like my mother, who would protect the elephants? I had to be cunning, keep my wits about me, and come up with a plan.

I lie there squinting my eyes to appear asleep but watched what they were doing.

The fat man was pacing and yelling. His face reddened. Those piercing eyes narrowed into slits of fury.

"What do you mean they are gone? Where did they go? Find them! Bring them back! They have to guide us out of this God-forsaken jungle! We are not equipped for an extended stay here. They were supposed to guide us in, I would shoot my prey, and they would guide us back out to the waiting truck. And then we fly out of this place."

"Uncle," the young boy said carefully, "if the guides took off, there is no way that anyone will be able to find them. We will get lost if we split up. We should stay together. We could cut through the clearing and look for help for the lady. The elephants have left, so they won't trample us. We could try to find the path that we made coming in. Maybe we can get to the other side and then get help for her."

The large man looked furiously at the boy and fisted his hands. He raised a fist and shook it very close to the boy's face.

"Boy, have you looked around? We can't go into the clearing. That woman may be dead. If we didn't get her with the shot, surely the elephants have trampled her to death. Why would anyone in their right mind be in the middle of that herd anyway? She had a death wish, right boy?" The man grabbed the front of the boy's shirt. "It was her fault."

The boy visibly swallowed hard and took a step backward.

"Uncle, you shot her! She is probably dead. You probably killed that woman and this whole trip is sneaky and horrible. I feel awful for the woman. We should check on her. Maybe we can save her. We have to help her!"

The fat man that the boy called Uncle lifted the boy off the ground. He shook the boy so hard that fear and shock showed on the boy's face and he looked like he wanted to cry but didn't dare.

The boy's uncle spoke through gritted teeth. "The only people who need saving is us!" he said. "Now stop talking your nonsense and look around for our path." He released his grip on the boy and pushed him backward.

The boy tripped and hit the ground in front of me. His eyes widened in shock. The boy gave me a half smile and a half look of worriment when our eyes locked.

Suddenly, I felt a hard poke in my ribs by a rifle. It was the Scary-Face Man.

"Lookey who's awake," he said, grabbing my face in his large dirty hand and squeezing my cheeks together until my teeth cut into the sides of my mouth. I remained silent despite the pain and the watering of my eyes.

He grabbed me by the arm and hoisted me to my feet. I couldn't catch my balance and fell forward, landing by his boots. He kicked me hard in the ribs and I let out a grunt. The man sneered at me.

"Get up! Get up, you little spy!"

I curled myself into a fetal position to protect my stomach and ribs as much as I could. My body shook like I just got out of cold water, but it was just panic setting in.

The boy scurried over to where I was lying. He touched my arm and it brought me out of my thoughts.

"Can you walk?"

He put himself between my body and the man's boot. The boy placed a hand under my arm to help me up, and I tried to stand up straight, but my ribs hurt badly from the assault.

I was scuffed up, but able to walk. My arm, however, was very painful. I rubbed my shoulder, hoping for relief that didn't come.

The boy brushed dirt from my face and arms. He turned toward the Scary-Face Man. "Can't you see she's hurt? You can't fall that far without hurting something. It's lucky for her that she landed on you, Bain, or she would probably be dead. We would have two dead people on our hands," he said and then looked at me. "Where are you hurt?"

I didn't answer. My mind was moving as fast as a cheetah. I realized that if I didn't let the men know that I understood them, they would be more comfortable talking in front of me. I might be able to learn about their plans for me.

I began to talk in Swahili and was grateful to know the language that was foreign to these men. They didn't understand it when the guides spoke and called them lazy, so I knew it was a good plan.

I received blank stares from the group as I rubbed at my aching shoulder.

The Scary-Face Man loomed over me with a smirk on his ugly expression. Those deep red-purple scars looked fresh when he was up close. Like he recently got into a fight with a lion. He looked just mean enough to take on a lion and maybe win.

The boy looked at my face and peered down the length of me as he pulled a twig from my hair.

"You sure are dirty. I didn't expect you to have lighter skin. Look at you. You are covered in muck, and your knee is bleeding. Can you walk?"

I only stared at him as if I did not understand him. His brown eyes gave away his disbelief, but he didn't reveal what he expected.

"Can you understand me?" The boy looked me in the eye. I gave no sign of recognition, just continued to stare and speak a few Swahili words. Some of it was nonsense. I'd say things like, *what is your bedtime? Your sister looks like a hippo.* Stuff like that. I was right, no one knew the language, so to them, I was just a foreigner from the jungle who happened to have white skin.

The boy winked at me before he turned to look at his uncle. "She doesn't know what we are saying, I am sure of it. She is from around here. I think she was in the trees earlier. I thought I saw something following us, so it was probably her. She can't speak English, Uncle."

Uncle crouched down in front of me and glared at me.

"Are you sure she can't understand us? What is this little girl doing in a jungle and climbing through the trees? That's not even possible. Look at her. She's just a scrawny kid. How old are you girl?" He shouted as if I were deaf; his spit sprayed my face as he spoke.

"There is just no way she could survive out here all alone! I'm a grown man and don't think I could survive in the jungle for long. No, it is not possible. She must have other people around here. Maybe waiting to ambush us," Uncle said, grabbing my face and pointing his chubby finger dangerously close to my cheek as he whispered.

"If I find out that you can understand me, and you are lying to me, I will cut out your tongue and feed it to the hyenas!" His saliva showered my face, but I didn't dare wipe the drool away. Uncle glared into my eyes and looked for signs of fear from me, but I gave him nothing. I knew that fat man could never catch me as long as I made it to the trees. Then I remembered that my shoulder felt like it was out of joint and that I probably couldn't climb. It was another stroke of bad luck.

The boy put a hand under my arm to support me when I wobbled a little. "Well, we all saw her fall, so it is possible for her to climb in the trees. Maybe she was abandoned here in the jungle, or maybe she knew that woman in the field. Either way, she obviously knows this jungle."

Uncle slapped the boy on the back so hard it made him cough.

"Good thinking boy, find out what's wrong with her, fix her up, and we will use her to guide us out of this hell hole. It's as hot as hades here. We gotta get moving before I melt!"

Uncle grabbed a cloth from the back pocket of his pants and wiped the sweat from his neck and face. He pulled the old one from his shirt pocket and threw it toward the man they called Bain.

"Bain, fix her up and make sure she is secure. We don't want her getting away."

The man named Bain was the Scary-Face Man. He approached me, and I had to pretend that I did not know what Uncle had just said, so I just continued rubbing my arm and looking at the jungle floor. It was better to be submissive to dominant creatures. Never look them in the eye.

As Bain took hold of my arm, he sneered in my face and shoved the moist, sweaty rag into my mouth. It tasted of salty sweat and smelled terrible enough to make me gag.

"Hold her boy, this is going to hurt," he said, almost daring me to show some recognition that I understood.

If I was nothing else, I was stubborn and refused to show any acknowledgment as I choked on the rag. The man could do his worst. They had already injured or killed my mother, so there was nothing that they could do to me that would hurt me more.

The boy put a hand on my opposite shoulder and another one on my back to steady me, but I just stared straight ahead. I knew they could do greater harm to me than what was about to happen.

Bain probed his meaty fingers into my shoulder. The pain was excruciating, and I spat out the rag and swore in Swahili. No one in the group could understand me, so it was safe to swear.

I felt the boy's hands quiver. He looked away just seconds before Bain pulled my arm out straight and gave it a sharp tug.

I wanted to cry out, but I did not. One tear from the pain made its way down my cheek. Just one. I couldn't look weak.

When I heard a pop in my shoulder, there was a slight relief almost instantly.

The boy made a sling out of the smelly cloth and tied it around my neck. He helped me place my injured arm into the sling. I was thankful for his gentleness but didn't show it.

Bain approached me with a rope and tied it tightly around my waist. "Here you go," he said, throwing the other end of the rope at the boy. "You just got yourself an ugly little pet." Bain stepped back and looked me up and down. He wrinkled up his face with disgust and shoved me forward. "Dirty little brat." He shoved the boy for good measure. "Make sure she don't escape. Hear me, boy?"

Bain leaned in close and brought his face inches from the boy's scared eyes. "The way I reckon, she will naturally lead us to the way out. She will want out of this mosquito-infested bush just as quickly as the rest of us." Bain turned toward Uncle and placed his hand over the pistol belted on his hip. "We can figure out what to do with her later. I have no problem gettin' rid of these little monsters. We just need her to get us out of here as quick as possible," he said as he lit a cigar and blew the smoke into the air. "This should help keep those pesky biting pests from eatin' us alive." He smacked at his neck when a bug bit him. "Boy, tie that rope around your wrist. I'll make sure it's real tight. Cuz we don't want no brats gettin' away, now do we?"

Because Bain insisted on smoking those smelly cigars, he was giving away our location to any animal with a nose. He might be a big and bad person in the place where he came from, but not here. Here he is as vulnerable as a baby impala in a pride of hungry lions.

I found myself imagining that the insect bites would somehow paralyze him and that a big predator would come along and eat the scary man named Bain. There would be one less man to harm me, one less person to fear.

And that's when I thought of the perfect plan. If the men were going to hold me captive and make me lead them through the jungle, that's exactly what I would do. I would lead the group directly into the path of danger and let the jungle deal with them. I would follow my imaginary circle that extended out for miles. I could make sure they were all dead or lost before I ended up back at the spot where we started. I just hoped that Momma would survive long enough for me to get back, if she was still alive. I had to hope someone would find her before the lions or hyenas did.

I should have felt guilty about my plan to watch the men die. I was going to lead them to their untimely deaths. But the law of the jungle is always *eat or be eaten*, and I preferred to eat.

I had no plans to make the trip easy on anyone. Bain looked just evil enough to kill me once we reached their destination, so I had to get rid of all of them. *Kill or be killed* kept running through my mind—over and over again. I was about to do what I had to do to survive. It would be a challenge of predator versus prey, and I was going to be the one to set the stage.

CHAPTER 3

There were seven men left after the guide and the other two African men ran off. Uncle, Bain, and the boy were the key people, but there were four more who were always quietly following Uncle. They silently trailed his lead and never questioned his decisions.

I soon heard their names when Uncle barked out orders.

"Jasper, pick up half the gear. Since we no longer have anyone to do the heavy lifting, you two imbeciles will have to do it."

The man named Jasper shot a look at the other man and picked up some of the gear, leaving the bulkiest items for the other man. "The rest is yours, Clint. But if I were you, I would let old Otis and Lonnie carry some. They may be old as dirt, but they should be carrying their share," Jasper snickered.

I don't know why I even bothered to store the information; it wasn't that it mattered. But I have always been observant; even the slightest detail could show me who everyone was and how the men were connected.

Jasper was very skinny and tall. His nose was extremely long, and his nasal voice cracked when he spoke. He looked scared of everything, jumping at each sound or crawling thing he encountered. Jasper was always blowing his nose and sneezed excessively, making a lot of racket doing so.

The man named Clint was unusually short for a full-grown man. He wasn't any taller than me. I was five foot four. He kept his distance but had looked away every time Bain had mistreated me. I believe he was sensitive to my dilemma. It would be a shame to cause him to perish, but only the strong would survive this journey.

As Jasper said, Lonnie and Otis were very old men. They suffered more than anyone else in the group, as they struggled to keep up with the pace. I was sure that adding weight to each of them was going to make them easier targets for prey.

Jasper and Clint took up the rear of the single-file line we formed as we moved forward through the bush. I led the line, followed closely by the boy, Bain, Uncle, Otis, Lonnie, Jasper, and Clint. When the path became too thick, Bain would lead and chop our way through the foliage.

I studied the men to determine which ones were a threat. Jasper, Clint, Otis, and Lonnie were followers; like a wild pack of dogs, they were the omegas. They did as they were told and didn't question the leader.

The boy was smart for his age. His mind was always moving and he was quick to figure things out.

Uncle was the apparent leader, but he was weak. His excess weight caused visible signs of distress.

Bain was pure evil. I knew it and so did the boy. We could see it every time he looked at us. His eyes sent a shiver down my spine. He would shove the boy with his boot into the back of me if he thought that I was not leading them quick enough.

"Move it you two," he said as he pushed the boy into me.

I once stumbled, but the boy caught me before I fell. I liked the boy with his kind eyes and messy brown hair, almost the color of mine. His eyes were brown and his body tall and lean. He looked athletic, so if I had to run, I knew he'd be able to follow. I thought he might be able to catch me, or maybe just keep up with my pace. He walked very close behind me, because one end of the rope was tied around my waist and knotted in the back, and the other end remained tied around his wrist. Bain wanted to be sure that when they all slept, I wouldn't escape. I was their prisoner.

With my arm in a sling, I was sure that I could not climb a tree and swing to safety. My only option would have been to run through the jungle. But I wouldn't get very far with the boy attached to me. Unless, like me, he also wanted to run to freedom.

I tried to figure out how the boy fit into their story. No doubt, he was made to live with his uncle. I wondered why he didn't have a suitable family. There was, similarly, a sense of sadness in him that he suppressed. It showed in his eyes when he thought no one was looking. I wondered whether he saw the same thing when he looked at me.

There was also something special about him. It was almost comforting to be linked to him. I was thankful that if I had to be tied to someone in the group, that it was him. I had my best chance of getting away with him. He had no gun to shoot me, no weapon of any kind that I could tell.

I guessed his age to be about twelve-years-old. He could not have been much older. I had to hope that under those brown eyes there was someone who would be compassionate to my need to escape.

I needed time. Time to find the danger. Time to make sure that they were tired of the extreme amount of walking and the heat, and time to put them in a position of threat and get rid of them. One by one, I would watch them die. It wasn't difficult to find danger, it was always just around the next corner, just a few feet away, lurking in the shadows and judging when or if to attack. It was everywhere.

The group had no idea how to get out of jeopardy quickly by the looks of them, except for Bain. I imagined that he would just shoot his way out.

They were blind to the dangers as they passed poisonous plants, spiders, and snakes among others.

The rustle in the bush told me we were not alone. An unseen creature was stalking us.

The monkeys' warning cries confirmed my opinion, and I became tense and on alert for my own safety. I shifted my gaze back and forth, looking for the reason for the monkeys' calls.

Their warnings went unnoticed by Uncle, as he continued to push us to pick up the pace at the expense of further tiring the older men, Lonnie and Otis. They began to slow dramatically and the gap between them and the rest of the group was expanding.

Another few hours passed, and the rains began to hit the canopy above us, sending raindrops to the floor below. The darkness ensued, and the humidity rose.

The boy and I could handle the humidity better than the slowing group. We could move quickly. Bain seemed torn between staying behind with Uncle and the rest of the men and keeping up with us. He would pick up his pace one minute and fall back the next.

Uncle was beginning to tire. He held back the rest of the men. He was visibly suffering from his excessive weight and the heat. He was huffing and struggling to keep up with the stride I was setting. Lonnie and Otis were far behind. I lost sight of them. I wasn't sure how much harm they could do to me anyway, and I feared for them out here alone should they be left behind. But I couldn't think about that now.

The boy kept looking behind us as he pulled on the rope to let me know he wanted to say something. He made sure that we were out of earshot when he whispered, "My name is Tim. I wish I knew your name too. I am sorry." He cleared his throat. "Sorry for what happened to that lady. She was your mother, wasn't she?"

I turned to look at him, and maybe it was a look of worry or sadness that gave away my secret, but he figured out that I had understood them all the while pretending not to understand.

He smiled as I looked away quickly and kept my eyes on the path.

"I knew you could understand us. I just knew it! You are a tricky girl. And brave. Did anyone ever tell you that you are fearless?"

I only nodded slightly to let him know that I understood. Something about him told me that I could trust him to keep my secret safe. Maybe it was a child thing, the two of us being so close in age. Perhaps it was a survival thing. Having an ally both helped and hurt my chances. It was right that I should use my connection to him to try to escape. But if I started to care about his outcome, I would be risking my own.

But my turmoil ended when he spoke.

He gently pulled on the rope to get my attention. "You know I can't untie you, right? You know I can't let you go. I am pretty sure that they would kill me, especially Bain. And I don't think my uncle would stop him since he is stuck with me. You see, my parents died in an airplane crash two months ago and I was sent to live with my uncle. He is extremely rich and gets whatever he wants. This time, he wants the chance to shoot an elephant and keep its head to add to his hunting trophy walls. It's an entire room of animals that he or his friends have killed over the years."

"Uncle never wanted kids. He hates me. But I am his only living relative and he is mine. We are just kind of stuck with each other. Uncle is a rich businessman, so he is gone most of the time and leaves me with the maids. He thought this trip would toughen me up. I think he is hoping that it gets me killed. That way, he can get rid of me. He's sending me to a boarding school when we go back home—well, that is the story he told me—but I know differently. I don't want to go back. Uncle is mean and abusive, and I hate him."

I slowly nodded again as I ducked under a branch and pushed the foliage out of my way. I was right about Tim. He was with Uncle because he had to be, not because he wanted to be.

I never heard someone talk so much in my life. Maybe it was because I preferred the company of animals to humans. I guessed that Tim just needed to unload all the things that happened to him; I could respect that. I wished that I could do the same, but it wasn't safe.

Tim continued to talk low to ensure that nobody could hear us. "If I can protect you, Jungle Girl, I will. If I can free you, I will. I will try. I like you, Jungle Girl." Tim gave the rope a light tug, and I tugged it back.

It gave me hope. I began to think that maybe I wouldn't have to see that the boy died. Perhaps I could free him as well. Plans change. The way I saw it, he was just as much a prisoner as I was. Well, maybe not as much, but he was probably not in a good place if he had to spend the rest of his life with his abusive and dangerous uncle.

When I started thinking more about the plan I had been forming, it seemed to have some holes. If I could run away, and if they caught me, they might just risk being lost and kill me for attempting to escape. But, if I did nothing and led them to where I thought they needed to go, I would be killed anyway. If they found out that I was leading them in a circle, I was probably dead as well. The answer was simple. I had to try to go. The trees were my ticket out of danger if I could bear the pain. I would just need to go for it.

There was a sense of sadness in Tim's eyes that told me maybe, just maybe, he would run too. He might be able to help me climb. That plan would be worth thinking over if I had more time. But time was one thing I did not have, so I just reacted.

Even if I could untangle the knot in the rope, which was too tight to release, I knew that Tim couldn't survive in this place. Tim would be blamed for letting me go and would probably be beaten or worse. We had to be able to work as one unit. If we could move together, it just might work.

As we moved to an area with less dense foliage, I pulled on the rope and gestured with a nod toward the right. I held up three fingers. Tim turned pale as he realized I was going to make a run for it with him attached. The countdown started as I lifted one finger, then two. By the third, Tim was swallowing hard.

I took off like a shot, prepared for the resistance if Tim decided not to follow. I made up my mind that I would drag him behind me if I had to in order to free myself and get back to my mother. Nothing was going to stop me.

There was no resistance. Tim joined me on the dash to safety.

Uncle screamed. "Bain, grab her! Don't let her get away!"

Bain was fast, but I was faster. So was Tim. He ran with purpose and speed. If I was honest, I think he was faster than me.

My pulse was high from the adrenaline and the full-out pace of my run. I couldn't fail. I started the plan and put it into action. Now I needed distance.

I could hear Bain's pounding feet as he chased us. He swore through his gasps for breath.

It all came to a halt when Tim ran one way around a tree and I ran the other way. We collided when the rope tightened between us, sending us both backward. Our bodies struck one another; hard. The pressure from the impact and the rope tightness on my stomach squeezed the wind from my lungs. I tried to breathe, but no air made it into my lungs. I turned over onto my belly and gasped for air.

Bain was on us in no time. He grabbed me hard and shook me, lifting me off the ground by my shirt.

"Not so fast! You ain't goin' nowhere," he said as he grabbed a fist full of my hair and pulled so hard I thought he would rip it out by the roots. He dragged me back to the tree by my hair. Bain shoved me into it, striking my face into the tree. My teeth cut my lip. I could taste my blood pooling in my mouth. My tongue searched for missing teeth. Luckily, they were all intact. The impact bruised my cheek and it began to burn. I felt dazed for a moment as my eyes readjusted.

Uncle and the rest of the men caught up with us. Anger showed on Uncle's face right before he slapped me hard. It stung, but it didn't hurt as much as hitting the tree.

Tim stood and rubbed at his inflamed wrist, where the rope yanked him back.

"I tried to stop her, Uncle. She is a tricky one. So that's why I used the tree. It was sure to stop her if I made sure the tree was between us," Tim lied.

Bain snarled at Tim. "Looked like you were running away too, Boy. I think you were tryin' to help her escape, werntcha?"

Tim stood defiant. "I was trying to stop her. Why would I run away? I am part of this journey. I wouldn't betray family like that." Tim lied again to save his own skin. He did not even look ashamed, but darted his eyes away from my piercing gaze. I had to believe he did it to give us time; to let us live another day. But my next opportunity—if there was a next opportunity—would be difficult to come by.

Uncle stood in front of Tim for several seconds before he spoke. "Well, now that's real nice to hear, Boy. Such loyalty." The sarcasm dripped from his words. Uncle grabbed Tim by the arm. "If I were to get to thinkin' otherwise, well, I would just shoot you myself. Do we understand each other, Boy?"

"Yes, Sir," Tim answered, and he kept his eyes on the jungle floor as Uncle released him.

I didn't dare spit the blood from my mouth for fear that whatever was tracking us, would see me as injured prey and make me its target. I never wanted to be the weakest one. That's how predator's thought. Go for the weak.

I swallowed quickly and pressed my tongue to try to stop the bleeding.

Uncle grabbed the front of my shirt and spat in my face. "See if you can understand that," he said as his saliva ran down his chin. "You are nothing, Little Girl. Nothing, but trouble. Do not cross me again!"

He dropped me where I stood and glared at me for a few seconds before he turned away from me.

My plan was foiled, my escape ruined, and Tim's seeming betrayal. I wasn't off to a very good start.

We traveled until dusk. As the sun lowered, the men began to set up camp. Clint assembled tents as Jasper built a fire to cook their evening meal.

Uncle sat on a log with Otis and Lonnie and lit a cigar. "How many years we been doin' this?" Uncle stroked his chin in thought.

Otis scratched his head. "Musta been gone on forty years is all."

Lonnie joined the conversation. "Forty-two to be exact." He smiled.

Uncle took a long drag on his cigar. "Forty-two years, and we end up here in this shit hole. All for some ivory and the thrill." His eyes averted to mine.

I looked down as he continued. "Never shot a person before. Bain has, but not me. Seems like it's no different than anything else. We're all animals anyways, so it's no big deal. She was stupid, bein' in that field with those animals. Way I see it, we did her a favor. Way I see it, she was itchin' to get herself killed. Tell me, Boy, would you rather be trampled by a herd of elephants, slowly being crushed, feeling every bone in your body break and die slowly, or just be shot and die quickly?"

"I would prefer neither would happen to me." Tim drank from his canteen and avoided eye contact.

"Answer the question and look at me when I talk to you!" Uncle's temper was quick.

The boy looked up and swallowed hard. "I suppose the less painful choice would be the shooting."

Uncle, Lonnie, and Otis laughed hard. Uncle slapped his hand on his knee in delight. "Good to know, Boy. Good to know."

Tim would not even look at me and stopped communicating after the botched escape attempt. The way I saw it, he saved his own skin. If he would have followed me, we might be safe right now. At some point, the men were going to realize that I was not leading them to their destination. We were making one huge circle so that when I finally got rid of them, I would be close to home. When that happened, there was sure to be trouble.

I was tired and strained. Needing to reserve as much energy as I could, I just leaned against a tree and rested my eyes. Storing my strength and healing myself enough to get away had to be my only focus.

The calls from the jungle were like a sweet melody to me. It was a song that I have heard all of my life. I listened to the spotted hyena's cackle and the flapping of the night heron's wings as they found a branch to roost for the night. The hoot of the spotted eagle owl was just above me. I could hear the colobus monkeys nearby. It sounded like a sizable troop. There was intense fighting, which probably meant that one troop had invaded the space of another; they were very territorial. Leaves rained down as the monkeys jumped from tree to tree, screeching and biting. The pitch was deafening to those not attuned to the sound.

It was unnerving Jasper and Clint, who nervously look from each other to the trees, as they unloaded tin plates and forks from the gear. They kept speaking loud enough for everyone to hear how being in the jungle overnight was the last place any of them should be.

Bain set off around the perimeter of camp to find more wood for the fire. He came back and quickly stacked the logs and sticks before he settled back against a downed tree and took out a large knife. Bain began to feel the sharpness of the blade with his thumb and he stabbed the ground next to him.

"Gettin' mighty hungry," he bellowed.

Jasper and Clint served everyone, and we ate in silence.

Clint gave me a small amount of the bean concoction and some bread that was wrapped in a cloth. I hoped that it was not the rag that Uncle had used all day to wipe his sweat. The thought turned my stomach.

Clint also gave me some water, and I drank my fill as Tim handed me his banana. "*Asante*," I said and nodded to Tim.

"I guess that means thank you," he answered. "You are welcome." He gently pulled on the rope, but this time, I did not pull back.

After the meal, the men fed the fire so that it would last through most of the night.

Tim and I remained a short distance from it, sitting on the ground, still tied together. Tim was drawing in the dirt with a stick as I watched. He drew a tree, a person, and a face with a smile.

I kicked it with my boot, erasing the face.

Tim continued to draw. He drew a fat man that looked like it was supposed to be his uncle and he kicked it himself.

"Uncle, what do you think we should call her?" Tim asked as he drew a sad face over the happy one. I kicked that one too.

What difference does it make?" Uncle was chewing on a piece of jerky and drinking water, swatting at his arms that were being severely bitten by mosquitos. "They are eating me alive, these bugs! Give me another one of those Cubans, Bain. Maybe that will help. As far as the girl, you can name her anything you want. She doesn't understand you anyway, right?"

Bain handed him a cigar and Uncle bit off the end and spat it into the fire. He lit the cigar and took a huge inhale. The smoke he blew out encircled him in a cloudy smelly hue.

Uncle, always having to make all of the decisions, decided what to call me. "We will just call her Jane."

"Jane," Tim said. "I like it. Great call, Uncle."

"Well, don't get too used to her. It's not like she is going to be with us for too long."

Tim sat forward. "You aren't going to hurt her, are you, Uncle? You'll let her go when she is done leading us through the bush, right?"

Uncle smiled and took another long drag from the cigar. "I am not going to do anything. But, I can't promise that Bain will play nice." He chuckled and looked over at Bain, who was staring at me with his dark predatory eyes.

Bain rose. He came to stand in front of me and stroked my hair. "If you cleaned her up, she just might be a pretty little thing."

The men all laughed and I grabbed onto some leaves and vines lying on the ground, not knowing what he would do next.

"Now, Bain, control your urges. She can't be more than ten or twelve," Uncle exclaimed.

My eyes remained locked on the ground, but my hands began to shake, and I gulped. Bain took a swig from a flask he had in his shirt pocket. He spilled some of the liquid down the front of his shirt and wiped his mouth with the back of his hand. He crouched down in front of me, placed one hand under my chin, and lifted my face to meet his. The other hand, he put on my thigh, squeezing it.

"So, Jane," he scoffed through his crooked teeth. "Let's get one thing straight. I don't want no monkey business from the likes of you. You lead us out of this here jungle. And take us the quickest way out. If I even think you're doing anything I don't like, I will have to deal with you as a man deals with a disobedient little girl."

His face was so close that I could smell the alcohol and cigar on his breath. The stench of his sweat and poor hygiene made my stomach churn.

He slid his hand further up my thigh and gave it an even harder squeeze. Tim tried to yank the rope to move me closer to himself.

"Don't touch her!" He pulled hard on Bain's arm, only to receive a sharp slap along the side of his face. Tim rubbed at the bruise but continued to try to come between Bain and me.

"Uncle! Make him stop!" Tim's face was red from the slap and with anger, and he began to slap and punch Bain's arm.

Bain was momentarily distracted by Tim. He grabbed him by the hair, so I took the stick that Tim was using to draw in the dirt and I jammed it into Bain's leg. He let out a howl and punched me in the face so hard that my vision blurred before it knocked me out cold.

I am not sure if it was fear or exhaustion that took over, but I had what I can only describe as a vision. My mother was with me in a flowery field of light pink and fuchsia blooms. She sat with her legs stretched over the arm of an old, yellow-as-the-sun chair.

My father stood behind her in a white button-down shirt. Father looked so handsome as he looked down at us. And there was

Tim. He stood beside my father, all nice and clean, with his brown hair freshly brushed and parted on the side. My mother caressed his cheek as I laughed and laughed. We were all so very delighted.

My mother stood, and she looked so beautiful, with her crown of flowers that matched mine. Her sun-kissed hair was loose and flowing, like her dress. She picked me up, and I wrapped myself around her tightly, never wanting to let her go. I could smell her, I could hear her.

"Jane, wake up! You have to wake up now! Jane!"

CHAPTER 4

I gasped for air. I felt like I was falling and hitting the ground. My body jolted when I heard the sound. It drowned out the shrieking sounds of the monkeys and the cry of the hyenas with its thunderous roar. A noise so frightening that it vibrated in my chest and shook my knees. I knew that particular danger well, and I had successfully avoided it in the past by staying high in the trees. It was the lion's roar.

Everyone froze in silence as we heard it again. From the sound of him, I knew he was closing in on us. A terrifying sound, so deep that it extended out in a song heard for miles.

Lions were sneaky and lazy. They liked to surprise their victims so that they didn't have to work as hard. Well, the males anyway. The females were the hunters. They would use those dagger-like claws and their sharp teeth to take down their prey. But their roar was not as loud as the males.

Bain retreated to the other side of the fire and grabbed his rifle.

Tim and I got to our feet, poised for a quick exit. If we had to start running, I knew that he would have no idea what to do. Because everyone else was distracted, they didn't hear me whisper to Tim. "If we must, follow me up a tree. It's the only way that we can survive a lion. We have to get high enough that he can't follow. I mean really high."

That's when we heard the screaming. It was a blood-curdling cry, so terrifying the way it went from a scream to a gurgling sound, like someone was drowning. And then it stopped as quickly as it started. We could hear the sounds of bones breaking and flesh tearing off whomever the lion killed. At least the man didn't live long enough to suffer a great deal. The lion made speedy work of it.

The king of the beasts made all of the other animals hide.

I did a quick head count and realized that Clint was missing. Uncle noticed as well.

"Where is he?" Uncle dropped his cigar. "Where's Clint?"

Jasper was visibly shaking. "He went to take a wiz. That was about ten minutes ago. I guess he never came back." Jasper was averting eye contact with all of the men.

"You guess?" Uncle said and began to pace.

Jasper began to move closer to the fire and picked up a stick that was burning on one end. He glanced into the bush, looking for the predator.

"I mean, he just sort of said, I'll be right back, I gotta relieve myself, and then I guess he didn't come back. I was too busy with the gear to notice," Jasper said carefully.

Uncle began to bark out orders.

"Bain, secure the perimeter. Jasper, get fires going all around us. Maybe we can scare him away. Boy, get you and Jane closer to the fire. Men, we will take our watches every two hours. Between all of us, we should be able to ward off anything that wants to eat us."

Bain stood with his gun positioned in front of him and looked convinced that the statement was true. Jasper did not.

"Sir, shouldn't we look to get higher? That girl, Jane, she was in the trees. Maybe that's where we are the safest."

Uncle was annoyed. "Ever sleep in a tree, nit-wit? I am sure you haven't. And I am not climbing up some dumb tree when we have plenty of rifles and ammunition. Think, man, think! I swear you don't use the brains you were given at birth."

Jasper backed down from the conversation. No one spoke another word that questioned the decision of the leader. But Jasper was right. It *was* much safer in the trees.

It was almost dawn before we felt that the danger subsided and we could move from our location. With the men taking turns keeping guard, Tim and I could rest against a tree. When we woke, the men were busy tearing down the camp. They were not paying any attention to us, so I took the opportunity to give information to Tim that I knew he was wondering since we met.

I grabbed a stick and wrote one word for only Tim to see. *Zura.*

"Zura?" he whispered, as I pointed at it again. "Ah, it's your real name, right?"

I nodded at him, and he smiled. "It's nice. I have a pretend jungle sister if only for a short time and her name is Zura. You can be my sister from the wild. The jungle princess."

I used my uninjured hand to wipe my message from the view of anyone else.

The two of us bonded out of the situation and a like-minded need to stay alive; Tim and I were siblings for that short moment in time, and neither one was alone. It gave us the strength to know that we had each other's back. At least, I hoped that I could trust him.

"Zura, I'm going to protect you, I promise you," he said as he touched my tender cheek where Bain had punched me. "I am sorry that I betrayed you. I was just so scared of my uncle. I never had a sister or a brother for that matter. But if I did, I would want her to be brave just like you."

Jasper and Bain hurried with the chore of gathering the supplies, while Uncle was brushing crumbs off his distended belly. He handed some of the food to Otis and Lonnie. He continued to eat what looked like a cake of some sort. My stomach growled in protest.

I knew perfectly well that Uncle was not the sharing type. He wasted crumbs as he gorged himself. Crumbs that I would have happily eaten. And when he spoke, he sprayed cake into the air.

"Well, let's make sure it's safe before we see what damage was done to Clint," he mumbled through the crumbs.

Tim's eyes grew big as he sat forward in fear. "We are going to look for his dead body?"

"Well, yes, we are going to look for his dead body. Wouldn't you want someone to look for your dead body?" Uncle shook his head as he continued to eat.

"I am hoping not to *be* a dead body."

"That remains to be seen. Keep sassing me with that attitude and I can promise you, you *will* be." Uncle's threat was real.

Tim remained silent as we packed up the small blanket they allowed us to share, and we started to move in the direction that Clint went the night before.

Jasper led the way this time.

"I saw him go this way," he said, pointing in the direction of very dense vegetation.

The body wasn't hard to spot, but it was easy to turn a gaze in another direction. The lion had devoured Clint's internal organs, and his body was covered in flies. Clint's neck appeared broken, and a large chunk was missing. That's how lions kill. They go for the throat. That explained the gurgling sound we heard the night before. He drowned in his own blood if he wasn't dead before the lion started to eat him. Lions don't wait until the prey is dead before they begin to consume their prey. Lions do not waste time, period.

I noticed that one of his legs was also missing. I had witnessed several times what a lion could do when he feeds. They'll eat their fill, then, if the prey is too large to drag away, they'll take part of it and hide it for a later meal. but I'd never see it this close up—and never on a human. But at the end of the day, humans also followed the jungle rule, *eat or be eaten.* Humans are not always at the top of the food chain.

Tim was throwing up in the nearby bushes.

"Weak," Uncle said. "Weak like your father. My brother never had the stomach for death either. Couldn't hurt a fly, Lionel was weak. Such a mama's boy."

Jasper found the courage to speak up in Tim's defense. "He's just a little boy. Can't be more than eleven or twelve. I want to throw up myself."

Bain shoved Jasper out of the way.

"Because you are weak too," Bain said as he bent down to look at Clint's body and tapped it with his boot as he stood. "Want me to dig a hole, Boss?" Bain had no compassion for anything dead or alive.

"No, leave him." Uncle began to walk away.

Jasper's head shot up. "Wa-we are just going to le-leave him?"

Uncle stopped and turned as he gave a disgusted look to Jasper.

"Yes. Clint is part of the jungle now. Let the wildlife do away with the evidence. We gotta go. We don't want that lion to find us near his kill."

He certainly was part of the jungle now. He would be eaten by anything that could get a hold of him. Then the predators would defecate, and he would become part of the ground. Though I knew I should be happy that I had one less man to deal with, I was not. His death bothered me. His death was senseless. And Clint had not been a real threat to me because of his age and frailty.

The next time we rested, it was mid-afternoon. We made our way to the river. It was not a very deep part of the river or very wide, but it was fast running. Everyone drenched themselves in the brownish water. It felt wonderful to splash my face and arms, but I did not dare to drink it. It was always safer to boil the water before you drink. If they still had their guides, the men would have known it. The microbes in this water could kill you. And the bush was no place to become sick.

As Tim cupped his hand to take a drink, I grabbed his arm to lower them from his lips and shook my head. I whispered, "boil," and he understood. He filled a metal container from the gear and began to build a fire. We were desperate for a drink but waited until the water was boiled and drank it as it cooled. I added the leave from the rooibos tree to make us a tea. I handed a silver cup full of tea to Tim.

"Drink," I whispered. "It is full of vitamins. It will help you stay strong."

We both sipped our tea as Bain watched. "Make sure she don't poison you, boy. She'll put some poisonous plant in there that'll stop your heart." Bain mocked, as he continued to drink from his flask. I was pretty sure it wasn't water.

I handed Tim some of the Rooibos leaves before I placed a handful of leaves in the pocket of my shorts. I kept a few out and demonstrated to Tim to put the leaves on his cuts. I placed a few on my knee in hopes of stopping the burning sensation and another handful on my swollen eye and cheek, where Bain had punched me.

Uncle, Jasper, and Bain became abnormally quiet. That scared me. Tim also took notice, and he nudged me.

"What do you think that is about?"

I only shrugged.

The men came to sit by the fire across from us, for a rest and to dry their clothes. They all stared at me with looks of dislike.

Uncle cleared his throat. "I suspect we should be nearing the truck sight soon, right Bain? I suspect that we don't have much further to go until we get to where we started this trip. My ride will be waiting for us. We can get out of this disgusting hole-in-the-earth and never return. Too bad our group has dwindled a bit. But when it is your time to go, you go. Clint is in a better place, right, Boy?" Uncle drank deep from the canteen that he filled with the questionable water from the river.

I hoped it rendered him helpless with intestinal troubles. This was not the time that anyone would want to have that sort of issue. But if I wanted anyone of them to go, it was the leader.

We continued on our passage until the heavens began to darken from the approaching storm. Uncle signaled for everyone to stop. He was limping slightly like one leg was longer than the other. Several times it looked as if he would trip, but he caught himself every time.

Uncle sat on a downed tree and took off his shoes to inspect his feet. They were beginning to swell. He tried to rub them but could not reach over his excessive girth.

"Boy, get over here and rub my feet for me," Uncle bellowed.

Tim looked panicked as he made his way over to Uncle, with me in tow. Up close, his feet were nasty, with his too long toenails that looked more like talons than nails. The nails were yellow and thick looking, growing into points. His foot was visibly swollen, turning purple around his ankle. His blue veins looked as if they would burst at any moment.

Tim looked as though he would become ill. He swallowed hard and took in a deep breath. Tim held his breath and turned his head away while he began to rub Uncle's swollen smelly feet.

Uncle took delight in the rubbing and closed his eyes. "Aah," he said. "Finally found something you are good at; rubbin' feet."

Uncle was putting his socks back on his feet and I couldn't help but stare at his enormity. It was hard to imagine that this overweight man could get any bigger. He was out of breath and his hands were shaking.

"Give me my water, Boy."

Tim picked up the canteen and handed it to his uncle. "Are you alright, Uncle? You don't look good and you are sweating badly. Do you feel ill?"

"Well, of course I don't look good. I'm sweating from this heat, and we are in the middle of a gosh-dern jungle," Uncle said as he wiped his cloth over his beet-red face and neck. Uncle glared at me. "What are you looking at, Jane? Never see a man sweat before? Why anyone would choose to live in a place like this, I will never know. It's only good for hunting and game. And even that got screwed up. Dumb broad getting in the way of a good shot. Women are only good for one thing, and that's tending to the needs of men. Ain't that right, Bain?"

Bain let out a grunt and nodded.

I knew he was testing me again, looking for a sign that I could understand him by insulting my mother. It was difficult, but I bit down on my tongue to keep from speaking out.

I had to look away from Uncle. The man turned my stomach. He was vile and callous. I chose to ignore their taunts and focus on my surroundings. I could never lose track of our environment. I needed to be aware of danger, so that if Tim and I would have to make a mad dash to safety, I was ready. As I surveyed the perimeter, a movement caught my eye and I froze. It was the slightest stir in the brushwood. Long, and the color of the sky just before the rains come. Dark gray and terrifying, smooth and flat, it crawled closer and closer to its victim. It looked to be about ten feet long. It would be unusual for it to bite a human, but one bite would kill a grown man in a matter of hours, maybe even minutes, without proper care. It was a black mamba, a formidable enemy with fangs that could strike fear into anyone's soul.

It slithered its way onto the log that Jasper was occupying.

Jasper was oblivious to the snake. He sat on the log, listening to the men talking about all the things that they thought women were good for, and I didn't understand most of the conversation. I had a feeling that it was probably better not to know.

Jasper smiled at their vulgar conversation. As he turned to look at Uncle, he moved his hand down onto the snake. The menacing creature made his strike, attaching itself to Jasper's arm just above the wrist, pumping it's venom into Jasper's limb.

Jasper's high-pitched scream and flailing arms made him look comical. But there was nothing funny about his situation. He was going to die. He viciously continued to try to free himself from the serpent's clamped jaws. His long arms continued to move around, and the snake held tight.

Bain progressed quickly, grabbing the snake by the tail. With one swift blow of his knife, he beheaded it, but it remained attached and continued to pour toxins into Jasper's body.

Jasper sat down after the dead snake released its grip. But he continued to yell and shake in his panicked state.

"What kind of snake was that? Does anybody know? Do you know, Jane? You have to know! Am I going to die? I can't die like this. I don't want to become part of this jungle like Clint. I don't want no animals scraping me out," he said as he rose and cornered me against a tree. Jasper grabbed me hard by the arms and caused my injured shoulder to throb. I could only stare at him. Of course I knew what type of snake bit him. I also knew that the outlook for Jasper to last more than a few hours was doubtful.

Uncle shot up from his seat. "Will you stop your blasted yelling? Do you want to alert every predator to our location? You are going to get us all killed! If you don't stop that shouting immediately, I will have Bain just shoot you now, and you won't have to worry about a little snake bite. The likelihood that you got bit by a poisonous snake is improbable."

Jasper shook his head but lowered his tone. "Improbable if I am sitting in my backyard in Chicago, and a garter snake bites me, more probable when I am in a jungle surrounded by all kinds of dangerous creatures."

Uncle was not deterred from his opinion. "Pull yourself together. We will have it looked at once we get out of this blasted jungle. Now let's get moving!"

Uncle leaned forward to look me in the eye, and he spat in my face as he spoke. "Jane, for your sake, the end of this trip better be soon," he said with a gleam in his eye as evil as that snake.

CHAPTER 5

It made me very nervous that we were almost full circle from where we started and there were still men very much alive. I didn't plan the path well enough. The circle wasn't as big as I thought it would be and I was running out of time.

Not as much time as Jasper was running out of with the venom doing its work. Maybe I should have felt sad or guilty because I knew Jasper would die. But with a bite from a black mamba, getting help was crucial. There was no helping him, and it was his stupidity that would cause his death, not me. My only crime was not telling him to watch out.

As time ticked forward, Jasper began to show the first signs of the poison streaming through his body. He complained of a headache and said that there was a metallic taste in his mouth. Jasper stopped and had to sit down. Before sitting on the log, he checked it for signs of snakes and any other danger. "Boy, hand me some water," Jasper whispered as he rubbed his temples.

Jasper opened a case of medical supplies and swallowed two white, round pills with the water. The sweat just poured out of him and his hands shook. He began to salivate—another bad sign. He used his sleeve to wipe the drool from his chin.

Jasper had the look of a defeated man. He knew as well as I did that his time on this earth was very limited.

"My arm feels numb where that evil snake bit me. Maybe that's a good sign," he wished out loud.

I knew it was not a good sign. It was a bad sign. It meant that the poison was progressing.

Bain placed a tourniquet on the bite as tight as Jasper could handle the pressure. They tried to stop the spread of poison.

Bain handed his flask to Jasper. "Here, take a swig," Bain said.

He gulped the amber liquid. "Thanks."

His condition halted the group from continuing our journey. But we had to stop until he passed. It was saddening to sit and wait for someone to die, but that was precisely what we did.

Bain made a fire, Uncle gave Tim and me two apples from the supply rations, and Jasper laid on the ground with a blanket under his head.

Bain threw a blanket for Tim and me to share. We worked together to spread it out on the ground. Tim and I laid there silently listening to the sounds of the jungle and Jasper's labored breathing and moaning.

Hours passed into the very early morning. The rain began to trickle through the trees. I allowed the droplets to stay on my skin and enjoyed the light mist soaking my clothes.

Jasper held on as long as he could. Eventually, the toxins took his life with one last release of energy. He let out a final rush of air, his eyes were fixed on the sky and his mouth hung open.

Bain, who was standing guard, walked over to Jasper's expired body and kicked at his boots. He announced his death without an ounce of compassion.

"Well, that's over. It will be light in a few hours, might as well rest for a spell."

It was too early in the morning for us to travel, so I tried to get a few more hours of sleep. All I could think about was a dead body lying close to us, getting myself home, and my mother's face before I drifted off.

My mother came to me in my dream. She and I locked so tightly together in a hug that felt so real. She held me as I cried, and she dried my tears with her long, flowing dress. Our flower crowns were still intact, not a petal out of place. We sat in my imaginary garden of pink and fuchsia flowers, and she sang to me. It was a lullaby that she used to sing to me to help me go to sleep. Momma rocked back and forth, pulling me close. The gentle sway was calming, and I hugged her tight.

I cried because it all felt so real. I missed her.

I couldn't tell if she was visiting me in a dream, whether she was an angel visiting from heaven, or alive and thinking of me. I let out the hurt and pain and terror that encircled me. My tears flowed like a raging river.

There would never be a bond greater than the love a mother had for her child. She spoke in a whisper.

"Zura, please don't cry. I know that I have always told you not to be reckless. I want you to forget that. Forget that I said that you would be responsible for giving me a heart attack. Forget when I said to be more like a lady. Be a warrior. Just do what your father has always told you. Be fearless. Fearless as your father knows you are, like I know you are. Please, be courageous. Come back home, Zura. I miss you."

I woke as Tim tried to comfort me.

He whispered, "Zura, I am going to get you out of here and get you home, please don't cry. I will find a way. I'll get you out."

I dried my tears with the dirty sling that remained wrapped around my neck. It looked to be the cleanest part of me. Not trusting my shoulder, I had to see whether I could use my arm, so I removed it from the sling but kept the cloth tied around my neck.

The camp was noisy with the snoring men. The only person that I couldn't see was Lonnie, so I assumed he was somewhere keeping watch.

Tim was very close to me and only spoke softly. "Are you better now Zura?" Tim said. "Did you cry it all out?" he whispered. "As I said, I will get you out of this, I promise."

I dried my tears one last time and I turned to face him. I knew the boy had no more idea how to survive in the jungle than the grown men. I had a feeling that if I didn't also rescue him, the men would kill him and leave his body to rot in the jungle. I could only think that way because of how terrible they treated him. I knew that I was his only hope. My knowledge of the jungle would be the only reason that Tim survived.

"No," I told Tim. "I am going to get *you* out."

Jasper's death caused an echo of silence over the remaining group. Jasper was a faithful follower in life, and it led him to his grave. Just like Clint, we left him there as food for nature. Just like Clint, it should have relieved me to know that I only had four more men to rid myself of so Tim and I would be free, but it didn't. A necessary evil was what was happening. I knew that I could not control the choices that the men made in following Uncle. Their poor decisions caused them to pay the ultimate sacrifice—their lives.

The next morning, we set out again. I led the way, followed by Tim, Bain, and Uncle. Lonnie and Otis were not too far behind for me to see, but Uncle didn't stop pushing us forward, refusing to slow our pace. He limped heavily, but kept up.

From the look of them, Lonnie and Otis were significantly declining. They struggled to breathe and used walking sticks to help them manage the terrain.

Under fallen trees, over large limbs and through dense foliage, I created an invisible path that went right back in the same direction that we left. They never noticed that the scenery was almost the same, because we came at it in the other direction, so it made sense to me that they couldn't see what was right in front of them.

If I had to feel sorry for anyone else on the trip besides Tim and me, it was Lonnie and Otis.

Lonnie was much older than the rest of the men. And he looked worse for wear, with his filthy tan pants half tucked into his high boots. His stained loose-fitting shirt was neither tucked in nor out. It hung off his feeble body. His gray and black scruffy beard made him look destitute. But, he had kinder eyes than the rest of the men. They were warm and brown and full of life's experiences. He smiled more than the rest too. It made him look worldly and even sympathetic at times.

Otis was gruff. His boisterous voice made it impossible to tune him out. His slicked back hair began to hang in his face in black ribbons, and Otis smelled incredibly bad of body odor. In my imagination, I could picture waves of vapors exuding from him. I could see thick puffs of foul-smelling smoke lifting from his body and into the air. It was like an open wound that continuously bleeds.

Otis wiped his forehead and used the water from his canteen to wet the rag. He placed it on the back of his neck. "Could it get any hotter and stickier? I reckon we'll all be cooked from the inside out unless we get out soon," he said as he adjusted the leather pouch on his back with a loud grunt.

Uncle was in a foul mood, so Tim and I put as much distance between us as we could.

Uncle was not in the mood to hear any complaining from any of the men. He grumbled as he drank more of the water and rubbed his stomach. This time his target was Otis.

"Yes, it can get hotter, you imbecile, this is Africa! Now we have to figure out where the truck will be. This field is a clearing in the jungle, and we were gone about the same time as we traveled in. It's gotta be close."

"That makes no sense." Otis countered. "You've lost your marbles."

Uncle's face was hard as stone. He did not tolerate anyone questioning his authority. Uncle drank more of the tainted water before he addressed Otis. "What do you mean it makes no sense? Makes perfect sense. Spit it out if you have more to say, let's hear it!"

Otis's face showed his irritation with Uncle, and he readjusted the heavy pack on his back.

"Did you ever tell the girl where we need to go? Ever stop to think that we relied on those guides to get us in without question? We never thought something might go wrong and that we should mark the trail or something. If we don't know exactly where we are going, how does she? How the heck would she ever know where the truck will be parked? She couldn't understand us even if we did tell her. You have been blindly following her for days. God knows where she is leading us. She could lead us to hell and we'd never know. It feels hot enough. We might just be there already!" Sarcasm dripped from his words like the sweat off his body.

"And exactly how was I to tell the little heathen where we are heading? I didn't know myself. The whole thing was supposed to be hush-hush. A favor for me from some important people here in Africa. Next time, Otis, I'll not invite you. You can miss out on the trip of a lifetime. And if you keep it up, you'll find yourself wearing a pair of cement shoes at the bottom of the river."

"You threaten me after all these years? That's just despicable. A next time? You assume we *get* a next time. Look around. We aren't exactly the bee's knees right now, are we?"

Otis paced with his hands in his pockets, looking at the jungle floor, and using his boots to crush any bug that moved.

"And another thing, you're logic is all wet! Again, how does a girl who we cannot even communicate with know where to take us? We were so scared after you shot the woman that we just wanted to get away without a plan as to how we get to where we need to go. So much for your leadership!"

Both men had reached their limit.

Lonnie calmly tried to add his opinion. "Now, now, gentlemen. That's not very helpful to get all balled up. This whole conversation is baloney and unproductive. We are intelligent, wealthy men. Surely we can figure this out calmly and rationally."

Uncle always had to have the last word. He turned from Otis and started to catch up with Tim and me.

"Anyway, we lost too much time on the Jasper thing."

Tim perked up and stopped dead in his tracks.

"The Jasper thing? Another man has died. Are you that callous, Uncle?"

Uncle was in no condition to tolerate back talk from Tim.

"I'll not have you second-guessin' me or speakin' out of turn. Children should be silent. Children should be seen and not heard! And if you want to continue to be seen, you'll shut that trap of yours and mind your manners!"

Uncle rubbed at his side, and he had a look of pain on his face.

"It's phonus balonus, that's what that is."

I knew that Tim was trespassing on dangerous territory, so I diverted their attention by speaking Swahili in a loud, exaggerated voice. We finally reached the grassy field. The same field that Momma's new elephants liked to graze. The same herd that took Tembo in when he was orphaned. That same area where I saw my mother fall. So close to Wild Hearts, yet too far away for me to sprint and not be followed.

I anxiously searched the landscape for her, but it was too difficult to see anything through the tall grass. I called out to her in my mind. *Please give me a sign so that I know you are alright. Please, Momma. You come to visit me in my dreams, now see me in life. I need you. I love you. Send me a sign. I am so scared, Momma.*

I couldn't let my mind go any further into my emotions. They made me weak, and my mother wanted me to be strong, to be fearless like she said. That's what I had to keep reminding myself. I had to hope that she was alive and that I would see her again soon.

I was surprised that no one realized that we were facing the same field that started the journey. The path I took had changed slightly, and we were not in the exact spot, but almost. Nothing was remotely familiar to Uncle; at least he didn't say so. I was sure that if any of them expected that I led them back to the beginning of our journey, they would have killed me. Those evil men would have left my bones to rot in the jungle.

Tim pulled on the rope to get my attention. "What are they?" He pointed into the field. The other men were too close for me to answer him. I remained silent but noted that it was a perfect place and time for another demise.

Anyone who spends time with wildlife sees the beauty and danger of the moment when prey suddenly realize that they are being hunted. A look of shock and worriment show in their eyes and their movements become scattered. The predator's vision is intense as they focus on their prize. Like a storm's black clouds that blow and circle in the sky with its temper, its threatening force gives way to the impending storm. There were signs, always signs. You just had to be observant and know what to look for; nature was the ultimate camouflage.

Wildebeests by the hundreds grazed near a small waterhole. Those that couldn't drink would eat. Some did neither. They were the lookouts, searching for any potential harm to the herd.

The herd was on its migration trail, always searching for food and water. They traveled over hundreds of miles, causing the older, sick, and the young to fall victim to predators.

The blue wildebeest, with its sizeable stocky body, silver-gray color, darker vertical stripes, and its massive curved horns is a white-bearded animal, part of the antelope species. Full grown, wildebeest could do a lot of damage if they wanted to. Even the lions do not tangle with the adults unless they must because it's a dangerous decision. And unlike humans, animals don't kill for sport.

When wildebeest face danger, they send out their alarm calls, alerting the herd of a threat. This herd was in constant motion, and the guards were standing erect. The guards bellowed out at the sight of female lions. The presence of the lions made the herd very nervous. The wildebeests grunted and made snorting sounds to try to intimidate the predators that stalked them.

The lions lazily assembled under a tree, waiting for an opportunity to present itself. The skill and power of the lionesses were astounding. They searched out the weak and the young, just like Uncle and Bain. Always looking for weakness and then attacking. The men may not have sharp teeth, but they could do just as much damage and were just as dangerous.

Eventually, someone was going to realize the deception. Sooner than later, I was going to be either beaten or killed for my trickery.

I moved away from the men and tried to assess the scene. I wanted to figure out how to cause a stampede or something to put the men in danger. Keeping Tim and me safe was my top priority.

Lonnie was the first to recognize the clearing. I saw him search the horizon and ground when everyone else was distracted with Uncle's tirade about needing more water, and who was going to give up their canteen for him to continue to drink since the wildebeests dirtied the water in front of us.

Lonnie picked up a bullet casing from the jungle floor. I became anxious as he started surveying the area even more and bent down to examine the very limb that sent me crashing to the ground. He came over to me and whispered.

"You are a tricky little one." He chuckled and secretly showed me the bullet casing. "Well played, Little One. Well played. Grown men aren't even as smart as you, but you already know that, don't you? I have a feeling you may want this. Wish I knew your real name," he said as he placed the bullet casing into my open hand and winked.

I slipped the casing into the pocket of my shorts. Lonnie patted me on the head.

"It may give you the encouragement that you need to get yourself home." He looked sadly into my eyes. "She was your mother, wasn't she?"

I blinked hard at him and he realized that I could understand them the whole time. He could not stop himself from laughing.

"You go finish this, Little Girl. Good for you, Jane, or whatever your name is. I'm too old for this. I'm too tired. And I am ashamed of my part in this," he said, and he turned from me and walked right out into the field shaking his head and laughing. I watched Lonnie go until he disappeared from my sight.

Otis, seeing Lonnie walk into the field started into it himself and stopped short when the massive beasts began snorting at him.

"Where's he going?" He looked at me. "He's going the wrong way, right, Jane? Well shoot, you're no help. What good are you, just standing there and watching him go out into that field? Why, he's gonna get himself dead on account of all them beasts. Not to mention the lions way over there under that tree." Otis scratched his head. "It don't make no sense. One minute he's talking to Jane and the next, he is laughing and walking out there. Crazy old coot. The sun musta baked his brains."

"How was he talking to Jane?" Bain perked up and questioned.

"Well, he was doing all the talking. Jane was just standing there and looking at him."

"Like she understood?" Bain scrutinized me suspiciously with those slits for eyes.

"How do I know? Ain't no mind reader. Lonnie was talking is all. And laughing like he'd gone mad. I can't see him any more through the beasts. Think he made it?"

Bain cocked his gun. "No telling, probably not. We best get out of here. Looks too dangerous to…"

His voice stopped as he eyed the area. He saw the limb that snapped when I fell. His eyes darted from the tree limb to the field and back to me.

"Why, you…" He walked toward me, holding his gun and pointing it at my chest.

"Stop!" Uncle shouted and pointed into the field. "Nobody moves a muscle."

Just then, the animal sounds intensified, and the lions stirred. They found their mark. It was impossible to know which animal they singled out in the herd of many. The female lions split up and began to stalk from different angles. The sound of the nervous wildebeest's movements was deafening. The dirt and mud from the rain began to cover their romping legs.

The lions patiently halted when needed.

Uncle began to yell.

"Boy, tell your pet there, Jane, that we have to go around! We can't be in the opening without any shelter. We are certainly not entering a fight between hungry lions and their prey."

Bain started toward me again but lowered his gun. "Sir, I think she's a liar."

"Quiet," Uncle whispered. "No sudden movements."

Tim played along, and I pretended that I couldn't have known what Uncle had just said. He pulled on the rope to guide me back into the jungle. I played along as well, acting as if I didn't understand. I heaved on the rope and walked just between the open grasslands and the protection of the trees. I knew what I needed. I needed the right tree and the right time. I needed a stampede.

I began to walk out into the clearing a little farther. Uncle shouted at Tim to stop me, just as Bain chased after me. And I ran. I sprinted hard and fast. And so did Tim. At one point, he passed me.

"Keep to the perimeter of the trees, Tim," I said when we were far enough away for no one to hear me. With Tim attached we were one unit, working together this time. "Climb!" I yelled as we reached the perfect climbing tree just within the perimeter, but with plenty of leaves for cover. "We have to get high," I told him, as I stretched and grabbed the first branch and kept an eye on the direction of the men.

The stampede began. With a swirl of activity, Bain, Otis, and Uncle were forced to wait. It was just the break that Tim and I needed to get high into the canopy and out of sight."

The noise grew and dust rose from their pounding hooves. The wildebeest sprinted through the clearing. They were running for their lives, just as we were, both trying to escape impending death.

The monkey's in the trees above us screeched as we invaded their space, but they did not attack. They were more concerned with the stampede and watching the lion's activity.

One of the lions stalked low in the grass, crouching down and moving forward. It jumped on top of the baby wildebeest. The wildebeest cried out as it tried to free itself. The lion reached out its massive paws to strike the wildebeest's leg and then its head. The lioness brought her prey down quickly, she turned the wildebeest's body to expose the baby's throat, and sunk her dangerously sharp teeth into the neck. Her jaws and mighty paws held on the bucking wildebeest. The young wildebeest was no match for the huntress, and it died quickly. There was no emotion tied to the killing. She didn't kill out of greed or anger or anything other than out of the need to eat. Eat or be eaten.

Tim moved behind me to hoist me up higher in the tree because I couldn't use my arm to its full strength. With each reach, I felt excruciating pain in my shoulder. I grasped the next branch and cried out, but continued to climb. Tim was behind me the whole time, pushing me and encouraging me.

"Zura, you can do this. You are strong, sister. Keep going! We are almost there."

By the time I reached the top, sweat from the pain had soaked my shirt. My arm spasmed from the extensions and muscle tears.

We positioned ourselves high in the canopy, away from the monkeys and out of harm's way—we hoped. I straddled the large thick limb and hugged tightly to the tree. Tim sat behind me and I rested my back on his chest. He surrounded me, protecting me from what was approaching, from *who* was approaching. I thought it must be Bain.

I saw movement in the bushes below and I grabbed Tim's arm in panic. The sight of the brown, gray, and white fur and large ears, and the animal's sniffing the ground and growling comforted me. That is when I relaxed my grip. Tim, however, tensed at the sight of him.

"It is alright," I whispered. "He's mine."

Tim did not relax. "Yours? What do you mean, yours?"

"He's my dog."

"That's a dog? Looks like a wild killer to me."

"Oh, he is. But, he is mine. Trust me. He is my fearless protector. Cha-cha will tear anyone apart who tries to hurt me. Just don't try to touch him. He'll rip your arm off," I whispered.

Tim shivered at the thought. "Good to know. I'm not going anywhere near that beast," Tim said, shifting behind me.

"That's probably best. Cha-cha doesn't like anybody but me. I saved him one day. He got too close to a leopard and almost died. I took him home and my father was furious, but he stitched him back together. He has been mine ever since. Just trust me."

"I do," he said and attempted to relax.

Cha-cha was crouched down in an attack position, ready to spring. He had found me and it renewed my spirit. It gave me hope. He must have been searching for me and tracking me with his keen sense of sight and smell, or he too was on the hunt like the lioness.

I slightly raised my hand to motion for him to stay. He obeyed. How delighted I was to see my wild dog. I wanted to get to him. He converted my fear to strength, and I knew that home was a few miles away, an easy climb for me. But not with my shoulder. I feared I would have to endure the pain to escape.

By the time Bain caught up with us, we were so well hidden in the tree, that he didn't see us. Motionless and holding on tightly, we watched him from our perch.

Bane searched the ground, shoving his gun barrel into any dark hole. He hunted the trees for signs of us. Bain raised his gun and pointed it as he scanned the canopy.

I didn't really have a plan as to how I should use Cha-cha, but I knew he would die to protect me. My fierce friend was a formidable hunter. And I knew that he could shred one of the men to pieces, but was he fast enough to kill all three of them without getting shot first? I wasn't sure, and that made me hesitate.

Uncle was out of breath when he and Otis caught up with Bain. And they were still arguing over whatever caused men to fight.

Uncle was looking a little green. He grabbed his side and groaned.

"We need to stop. I need something for my stomach. Must have been something I ate."

Or drank, I thought. Uncle consumed so much water, more than anyone else. I was right that it was teeming with bacteria. I did not doubt that the bacteria was raising havoc in Uncle's intestines.

"Stand watch you two. Those two have to be around here somewhere. Don't be afraid to shoot the boy, but leave the girl. We still need to get out of here. If she does this to us again, I'll beat her within an inch of her miserable little life." Uncle hobbled into the bush, I guessed, to relieve himself from the diarrhea pains that were sure to plague him.

Bain continued his examination of the area. He checked his rifle for ammunition.

"Fully loaded. That's all the permission that I needed. It's hunting time." He strapped his rifle over his shoulder and pulled his knife from its leather case around his waist to check the sharpness of the blade. Satisfied, he placed it back in its sheath. He checked his pistol for bullets and put the gun back in the holster before he faced Otis.

Otis's shirt dripped with sweat. He was gasping for breath and struggled to keep up with Bain. Otis was also visibly upset.

"If we are back where we started, as you claim, can't we just get to the other side of the field? That woman came from somewhere. There must be a home around here or a village. We could end this right now. I gotta get out of this jungle. If old Lonnie made it through those animals, then so can I. I'll be real quiet."

Bain shook his head. "You don't know from nothing. I would not do that. Those lions will eat you if the beasts don't trample you. What if the herd turns around to come back to the water? What would you do then?" Bain smugly stared at Otis.

"I'll make sure I stay close to the line of trees."

Otis dropped some of the supplies he was heaving around. He had been weighted down with more and more gear from the men who were now dead. And the extra weight had started to take its toll.

Bain stabbed his gun into the thick bushes, looking for Tim and me.

"You have no way of knowing whether old Lonnie made it, do you? He's probably a trampled broken body right now, being chewed on by those hyenas that followed the lions. And, by the way, you haven't been quiet one day in your life, Otis. You've been beating your gums since the day I met you. Better think it through. But I won't stop you, just so you know. I'm not responsible for saving your hide. I have my own fish to fry. That little brat has seen her last sunrise. When I catch her, I will put a bullet between her eyes. Sneaky brat."

"Warren said not to kill the girl, just the boy. Why he wants his only living relative dead, I'll never know. I kinda like that kid," Otis said. "He is no trouble. Smart too." Otis pushed his black, greasy hair out of his face and closed the gap between him and Bain.

"The girl may be a brat. The boy may also be a brat in your eyes. All kids are bratty to some degree. But they don't deserve to die. This trip got way out of hand. And those kids are smarter than all of us. You are mad because Jane made a fool out of you, out of me, out of all of us. She tricked us into thinking she was leading us out. But Jane made one amazing circle. Jane knew exactly what she was doing. I wouldn't be surprised if Jane understood every darn word we said on this trip. She's cunning. This jungle is her home. This is Jane's playground, and she just decided not to let you play in her sandbox. That just pisses you off, don't it?"

Bain's angered look intensified. Otis tauntingly stabbed at Bain's pride as a soldier, as a gunman. It made Bain look stupid.

"Trust me. This is no game. I guess you didn't know. This was more than a hunting expedition. It is also an elimination of some excess baggage. Warren is the big cheese and doesn't like anyone telling him what to do. When the courts made Tim his ward, he was furious. He never wanted kids and doesn't want to be strapped to one now who would inherit all his money. Especially the one that his brother had with that singer, Lorraine. He has other plans for that money, and so do I. I'll be lining my pockets with it, just you wait and see!

"My orders are clear, and the price is one million dollars to eliminate the boy. One little job and I am rich. And there's more. The girl will be another million, maybe two, now that she has made him look like a fool. I'm going to get a lot of dough. Nothing's going to get in the way of that."

Otis looked furious. "You're sick! Both of you are sick! Playing God with who lives and dies is despicable. I want no parts of this. I am out of here, just like Lonnie. I have a better chance with the wildebeest than with the two of you."

"Dry up, Otis, No one is stopping you. Go chase yourself!" Bain yelled.

Otis dropped the rest of the supplies he was heaving and readjusted the leather pack on his back.

"Say goodbye to Warren for me. I hope those kids win this deadly game of cat and mouse, and both of your bones rot in this jungle." Otis turned and began to walk toward the open field.

Bain only hesitated for a moment. "My bones won't rot here but yours will, you deserter." He lifted his rifle and a single shot rang out. Bain shot Otis with no more emotion than he showed for any of the other men.

Bain walked up to Otis' dead body. He was still fuming from the altercation. "Talk to me like that again," he said and shot Otis in the head. "Just to be sure." He walked away and continued his search for Tim and me.

CHAPTER 6

The monkeys went silent, the birds took flight, and Tim hugged me tightly.

"It's alright, Zura. It's alright," he whispered. We sat in stunned silence.

Uncle returned from the bush. He hurried his limping footsteps as he was zipping up his pants.

"What I wouldn't give for a john right now; crapping in the bushes is not ideal. What did you shoot? What did I miss? I heard the shots." Excitement showed on Uncle's face. "Hot dawg, did you bag the boy? Obviously, he was ungrateful and a traitor, running off with Jane like that. Where was he when you shot him?" Uncle stared silently at Bain.

"It's not exactly the boy that I shot," Bain answered.

"Not exactly? What does that mean? Tell me you weren't stupid and killed the girl too? I did hear two shots pretty close together."

"I didn't kill the girl either," Bain stated without emotion.

"What? Did you miss? You never miss. Mediocrity is not your game. Spit it out, man. Did you kill one of those lions or something? Maybe something that we can eat for supper?" Uncle started to peer into the shadowed trees nervously.

"No, I didn't kill a lion or anything that you are going to want to eat," Bain said dispassionately.

"Well, what were you shootin' at?" Uncle became irritated with the conversation. "Stop stalling and spit it out, you hard-boiled, lousy, good for nothin'!"

Uncle's eyes widened as he peered past Bain to the carnage on the ground. His hunting partner—his friend for most of his life—was lying face down with a bullet wound in his back and one in the back of his head. The first bullet pierced through the leather pack that Otis always wore while hunting. A pool of blood expanded out from Otis' body. The shot was directly in line with Otis' heart. Another bullet blew Otis' brains onto nearby bushes.

Uncle looked stunned into silence. I guessed that he never expected to see Otis dead on the jungle floor. Not that way. Not being shot by his man.

"What in tarnation happened here? Why in heaven would you be shooting old Otis?"

"Otis wanted to leave and he purposely agitated me into taking action. He was a deserter." An emotionally void Bain stood stone-faced. His military career trained him for killing. The war had damaged him and numbed him of all sensations when it had to do with death.

"I made sure Otis didn't suffer, but he was going off the deep end and I couldn't have him messing with my job. I already know I'm the fall guy here. I am going to need the dough to move somewhere else and start over."

Uncle's feelings were etched on his face. Shock, horror, and maybe just a little fear that quickly turned to anger showed on his pale expression. His glaring eyes, chalky appearance, and tight lips told just how angry he could be.

"Your job is to do what I tell you to do! Never did I say to kill my friends! What possessed you? You are not right. Don't hand me that line that he provoked you. We both know that it takes practically nothing to set you off." Uncle shook with anger and contempt, but his wrath halted as he grabbed his stomach and doubled over.

"Oh, man, this stomach issue is getting worse," he groaned. He started sweating profusely as his body tried to expel the toxins all at once. "We will finish this in a moment. Look for those kids while I take care of my intestines. And no more killing until I get back, understood?" Uncle scurried into the bush, not waiting for a response.

I kept an eye on Bain. I was still searching the landscape for any sign of Cha-cha. As quickly as Cha-cha had appeared, he had vanished.

I will never forget one day a year ago, after Tembo had moved on to his real family. I was practicing swinging from tree to tree, trying to work on my speed. The monkeys were rambunctious, hanging from vines and waiting for me to come close, only to block my path and throw off my rhythm. "Stop it, silly monkeys," I complained. "Can't you see I am trying to work on my swing?" In a split second, they halted their games and perked their ears to the sound. The screams of the dying prey came quickly, so I listened as well. There was a large cat in the jungle. The monkeys silently climbed higher, hiding themselves safely in the leaves, on limbs that would never support the weight of a big cat. If I had been smart, I would have followed their lead and climbed up higher, too. But I was too curious and inexperienced. I didn't know at the time that leopards are excellent tree-climbers. They can haul their prey up a tree with great strength and agility.

I had followed the sound and perched myself above the leopard. They were my favorite cats with their black spots mingled with the golden color of the sun. It reminded me of a sunset, combining light with dark to make a beautiful pattern. That coat made them unique and wanted by hunters who killed them for their fur.

I saw a wild painted dog approaching. The dog was skinny and a little silly looking with his large round ears and his thick fur made up of patches of gray, black, and tan. Either he was a young dog that was stupidly approaching a leopard with its fresh kill, or he was starving. Either way, the leopard never shares his meal with anyone, and he attacked the dog, grabbing him by the neck.

With a stroke of luck, or the cat just wanted to teach him a lesson, the dog was able to free himself, but not without some damage to his neck. I could see the bright red blood on the top of his fur. I wasn't sure whether it was coming from the dog or the fresh kill. Excitement had filled me to watch how nature decided who would live and who would die. That dog was a fighter, and he escaped.

The leopard looked torn as to whether to follow and kill the dog or continue eating the dead baboon. Choosing the path of least resistance, the leopard grabbed the dead baboon's carcass and jumped into the tree next to mine. We locked eyes. Those green-gray eyes looked as though they could pierce me, and I thought the cat would kill me right then and there. But he saw me as no real threat and hissed at me. I backed up, grabbing the vines next to me and swung away from him as fast as I could.

The whimpering of the dog and the blood he was spilling was sure to draw in more predators. He was as good as dead if he didn't stop his sound. I watched him shake his head and gasp for breath. He was struggling, and something about him made me want to help. Clearly, it was not a wise decision, but sometimes bad things turn into good things, and good deeds can lead to greatness.

I made sure that there was no danger around before I climbed down. My approach was cautious and slow. He was, after all, a wild and possibly dangerous creature.

I determined that he was young and inexperienced because he wasn't yet the size of a full-grown wild dog.

I crouched down near him, and he growled deep in his chest, but he did not show his teeth at me. Then something that could only be a miracle happened. He crawled to me, maybe in desperation. I cautiously pet his head, and he relaxed.

After I was sure that he wouldn't try to kill me, I picked him up and carried him back to my home.

I had a habit of trying to save every stray and injured animal in the jungle. Father's scowl did not deter me from placing the dog on the porch of our house.

"Rosie!" Father yelled for Momma. "No way, Zura. Here we go

again. It's not going to happen. Rosie!"

My mother appeared at the screen door. She stood there just watching me rubbing the head of that wild dog. I had his blood all over my hands, but I didn't care.

"Father, please! He is hurt. He needs to be stitched up, I think. A leopard attacked him."

"And just what were you doing anywhere near a leopard or a wild dog to know all of this?" Father was stern. "Rosie, reason with your daughter." He stood his ground and placed his hands on his hips.

Mother opened the screen door and kept a safe distance from the dog and me.

"Now, Zura, your father is right. You know how I feel about your adventures. Do you want to give me a heart attack?"

I rolled my eyes at her and sighed.

"No Momma, but he needs me. He is too young and stupid to make it on his own."

Momma folded her arms and gave me a stern look.

"And what's the rule of the jungle, Zura?"

"Kill or be killed. Eat or be eaten."

"And what does that mean?"

"It means that only the strong survive."

"And is this wild dog strong?"

"No, Momma, but he could be."

"Zura. No."

Father was losing his patience and approached the steps of the porch. The dog let out a warning growl and Father stopped.

I put my hand up to caution my father from approaching any closer.

"Stop! He is trying to protect me. That's all. He doesn't mean us any harm."

Mother chuckled. "He certainly has a sour personality, doesn't he?"

I laughed. "Yes, he does. I think I will call him Cha-cha." I said.

Momma laughed. "Very clever, Zura. Naming him the Swahili word for sour suits his personality."

Father began to pace. "Now you are on her side, Rosie?"

"Well, every child needs a dog. Didn't you have a dog as a child?"

"Sure. A Labrador. Not a wild beast."

"Well, we are not exactly surrounded by Labrador breeders here in the jungle, Peter." I could always count on her to give in.

Father walked away defeated. He returned in a few minutes with a long needle, and he handed it to me.

"Here. Give that beast this shot. Right on his hip."

"What is it?" I questioned.

"I can't very well stitch him up when he is awake. It's a tranquilizer."

I gave the shot to Cha-cha and rubbed his head until he fell asleep. I carried him into the animal hospital and watched my father stitch him up quickly.

Cha-cha was a unique creature and stood out at the sanctuary. Just like I stood out in Africa, with my pale skin. Though it tanned easily, it was not the shade of the people native to this country. But I am every bit as native to this land.

Cha-cha healed quickly and followed me when he wanted to. He also ignored me when he didn't want to be bothered. He was more wild than tame, and no other person could get near him. For some reason, he chose me as his. And he protected me as fiercely as if I were a bone.

Sometimes, he would disappear all day. I don't know where he went, but he always returned.

And he always showed up just in time to find me in a bad place.

I had to trust that his appearance was going to help Tim and I escape. Especially if Cha-cha was in a hunting mood and Bain was his prey.

Bain continued his search of the area. Tim and I remained utterly still in our hiding spot. After about twenty minutes in the vicinity, Bain took to calling out to me. As he turned his attention toward antagonizing me, I braced myself for the onslaught of reactions to his words.

"Don't get any funny ideas about escaping, Jane! I'll put a bullet in your heart like old Otis. Maybe I will kill the boy to slow you down. You can drag his corpse around with you, would you like that?" Bain walked off of the small barely visible path, into the thick perimeter. "Come out, or you will be responsible for both your deaths. Come out now, and you can save the boy! If you don't come out, his death will be your fault. Do you want to be responsible for killing him? Tell me, Jane. Was she your mother? That stupid woman in the field. She deserved to die, you know. I almost wish she was alive and came looking for you. That way I could have the pleasure of killing her. But I would make it slow. I would make it hurt so much she would be begging for death."

I tensed and, feeling my reaction, Tim covered my mouth with his hand.

"Don't respond," he said. "Don't you do it! That's what he wants. He wants to make you so mad that you speak out and reveal your location. Then he will kill us both, no matter what Uncle said to him. You heard him tell Otis what he planned to do."

I nodded my head to tell Tim that I understood, and he released his hand from my mouth.

"We can't let him win, Zura. We have to be tough. If I have to, I'll kill him myself." Tim took a brave stance. He lifted his chin and held tight to me and the branch.

Bain's search took him even deeper into the bush. We lost sight of him and began to relax. Eventually, his voice no longer carried on the light breeze.

I couldn't help but hope that Bain would be swallowed by a giant creature, like a great cat, or beat to death by an enormous, male, mountain gorilla. He deserved to be trampled by elephants or even speared by a rhino.

"Eat or be eaten. Kill or be killed," I said with my mind several miles away, home with my parents, having dinner, listening to stories and playing games.

It was comforting to lean against Tim. It was like going home to family, after a long day in the fields. It reminded me of my dream where Tim was with Father, Momma, and me. I thought about how well Tim fit into our pretty picture.

Tim's voice brought me back.

"What do you mean *eat or be eaten?*"

"Oh, it's the law of the jungle. Eat or be eaten. It means that you want to be the first to strike. You have to kill so that you can survive. That's what happens here. Momma taught me that when I was very little."

"Well, that's harsh."

"Life's harsh. The jungle's harsh. I mean look at us. Two kids in a tree and a man with a gun is chasing us. There is a dead man not fifty feet from this tree. That's harsh. That's not exactly how I planned my jungle time when I followed your group. You?"

"Not exactly. But since I already knew that Uncle wanted to get rid of me, I planned to find a way to get away from him. I was scared, though. You brought me courage. I saw the way you handled yourself when we found you, and I wanted to be brave just like you." Tim hugged me.

"I wasn't brave, Tim. I was scared. But I knew I had to survive. You see, it's because of my mother." A profound sadness expelled from my breath, and it cleansed my mind. There was no time for sorrow. I made a vow to have clear thinking and stay focused on my control. I had to believe that she was alive.

"I am so sorry about your mother, Zura." Tim cast his eyes downward.

"I know she is still alive because she visits me." I tried to mask the unbridled current of emotions.

"What do you mean she visits you?" Tim raised his eyebrow in disbelief. "How can your mother visit you?"

"In my dreams," I explained. "My mother comes to me when I am dreaming, and she tells me to be brave and fearless. I was so afraid that she didn't make it after being shot by Uncle. But she is alive, I just know it. That's why I have to get home. She needs me. I need her."

I could tell from the way Tim sighed, that he didn't believe me when I said that I saw my mother, but I didn't care. Something so vivid had to be real. Didn't it?

We waited until our patience was gone. Hunger, exhaustion, and dehydration led us to make a courageous decision to leave our safe space.

The gloomy sky darkened with thick, black clouds. The pitter-patter of rain hitting the leaves was a familiar melody of Mother Nature's song. It usually calmed me. I closed my eyes to the sound and soaked in the music.

Within minutes, we were covered in a blanket of rain. The shower pelting my skin was renewing. I lifted my head and opened my mouth to taste the clean, clear water droplets.

"Are you ready to climb down, Zura?" Tim whispered. "It's been a long time since we have seen or heard Bain or any sign of Uncle."

"Yes, I think it's safe," I told him.

Tim went first and helped me to climb down carefully. After we reached the ground, we hurried in the direction of my home. Long gone were the wildebeest, the lions, and the hyenas that occupied the field. I picked up the pace and began to run across the field to save time. We didn't get very far before Tim's foot fell into a hole in the ground. His leg twisted as he fell, making him scream out in pain.

His right leg was positioned at an unusual angle. Tim tried to get up, but only grimaced in pain. He yelled through his clenched teeth.

I was unable to stomach that raw look of agony on his face and the tears brimming his brown eyes. I just wanted that look to go away. But there was nothing I could do to ease the pain.

I helped lift Tim's foot out of the hole.

"Let me look at it," I said.

"No, let it go! Tim pulled away from my touch.

"Stop being a baby, Tim, and let me look at it!"

He shook his head, but I examined his ankle.

"Don't touch it," he complained.

"I have to examine it. Just try to relax. Or at least, try not to scream. You're going to give away our location." I quickly slipped his boot off of his foot and removed his sock. Tim's ankle looked bruised and it began to swell immediately.

"I don't think I can put pressure on it, Zura. You go on without me. Your mother needs you. Go!" Tim grabbed his ankle in pain.

"No! It's not broken, Tim. Just badly bruised. And I am not leaving you behind. We will both get home. Me and you, together. We are going home."

"I don't have a home!"

Tim's scars were not just superficial. He was hurting far more than his ankle, far more than being unwanted by his uncle. Tim suppressed the ache he had for his parents. Another bond to bind us.

"I know you miss your parents, Tim. And I am certainly not saying that mine could ever replace them. That would dishonor your parents' memory. I just want you to know that you can have a home. My parents will take you in and love you like their own. I just know it. I have to believe that Momma is alive, and she will want to hug your pains away." I leaned down and hugged him to comfort him.

The pair of us, still tied together, our clothes soaked through, were in the open and exposed to the world. We were missing our parents, missing our homes, our lives turned upside down.

Tim looked broken. Grieving for the parents that left him too soon, for a life he will never have with them. Tim let out his emotions in breaths of pain and fury. And I remained steadfast and silent, allowing him to feel the grief that he was unable to show before.

When Tim had cried it out, I lifted him up and supported his weight, not caring about my injuries. I was not going to let him down.

I pitied Tim and couldn't imagine what it was going to be like without him if he decided not to stay. Like my relationship with Tembo. When it came time to say goodbye, I wasn't sure if I could.

"We have to move," I said, and I led him back the short distance to the safety of the bushes.

The air was still and heavy with moisture from the rain. The animals scurried along the floor and high in the canopy of trees. I sat Tim down on a large bed of leaves, out of the rain as much as possible. Surveying the area, I looked for something to fashion into a crutch and found the perfect limb. It was smooth and angled at the top to fit under Tim's arm. The limb broke easily to the size we needed. "It's the best one that I could find," I said as I placed it next to Tim.

"It's fine. Come sit down and we will figure out what to do next." Tim said and patted the leaves beside him.

I pulled some berries from my pocket and gave them to Tim to eat.

"Do you have some for yourself?" he questioned, putting a few berries into his mouth and closing his eyes in enjoyment.

"Yep, I also found some grubs so I will be fine. Want to try one?" I held the fat squirming larva out to Tim.

"There's no way I'm ever eating *that*. Nuh-uh. No way, never."

"Never say never," I teased. "You never know what you'll eat when you are hungry enough. One of the things my father taught me when I was very young was what is edible and what I should avoid. He drilled it into my brain all of the time."

Tim ate the berries like he hadn't seen food for a year. I don't even think he took the time to chew.

I propped myself beside him, and he leaned on me. I ate a few berries myself, followed up with two grubs. They squished and squirted when I bit into them. They certainly didn't taste good, but they would help to give me energy for the trek ahead.

Tim shifted when he felt me twitch from the pressure he was putting on my shoulder.

"Sorry," he said. "I didn't mean to lean on your bad shoulder."

"It's alright."

No sooner did the words escape my lips that I felt the blow of Bain's rifle hitting the side of my head. I felt as though my brain had exploded when my neck snapped back in response to the shock. Fuzzy lights flashed in my vision. Stars danced before my eyes. There were a few seconds of dizzy confusion as my brain rattled inside my head. His voice was inaudible, though it began to clear as his heavy foot came down on Tim's chest.

Bain's face was only inches from mine. He unleashed his fury, biting, ripping the flesh from my bones. Bain's words cut deeply into the little space between us. "I got you now! Both of you are dead!"

CHAPTER 7

Tim struggled to breathe, his gasps of panic came sharply as Bain's boot ground into his chest. He positioned his rifle next to Tim's temple but he directed his hatred at me.

"You little brat. All this time you understood every word we said. Did you think we wouldn't find out? Did you!" Bain was becoming unhinged. The scary scars on his face looked deeper and darker with the flushed redness of his anger.

He lifted his heavy boot off Tim's chest, causing Tim to gasp for air and cough. He then redirected his hatred.

"All this time you, Boy, knew she was a liar. Whose side are you on, Boy? You are deceiving brats, the two of you!" Bain shook with rage, his face distorted to give him the look of a wild animal ready to impale the flesh of its victim.

"So, Jane, should I just shoot him now and let you drag his corpse around?" he taunted. "I am sure that will get the attention of a few predators, and I'll watch as they devour your lying heart."

Bain's malicious grin should have frightened me. It should have been a warning to me to keep quiet. I knew that he was serious, but it only fueled my hatred for him. It empowered me to want to fight back.

Bain continued his threats that no longer had me afraid. I reasoned that if he were going to shoot us, he would not have wasted time telling us about it. He would have just shot us like he killed Otis. Bain fed on fear. His kind of madness for power drove him to the edge of insanity. He taunted and threatened, but underneath it all, I believed that he knew he still needed me to get him out of the jungle. Otherwise, I would have been murdered in the jungle I loved.

Bain's eyes narrowed into slits. He scowled at me with a need for punishment.

"I know, Jane. Maybe I should just shoot *you* and let him drag you around. How far do you think he will get with your corpse dragging behind him? He is not exactly equipped to survive out here." Bain's hateful laugh made Tim visibly ill.

Bain eyed me as if I were his prey. "I could just kill you and free him from the rope and watch him try to find his way out. It could be a great game of cat and mouse. Only the cats in *this* world will eat him as soon as look at him."

Anger boiled up inside of me until I could no longer control my temper. I stood, and my vision swirled from the impact of the gun on the side of my head, but I braced myself for more.

"You kill either one of us and you will never get out of this jungle! Never!" I screamed.

Bain jabbed me so hard in the stomach with his rifle that I couldn't breathe, and I fell forward, landing on top of Tim.

Cha-cha leaped from his hiding place and attached himself to Bain's left arm above his wrist. Cha-cha's bite was so powerful that we heard the bone's break and Bain's eyes widened before his mouth opened into a howl of pain. He involuntarily dropped his rifle and it landed by Tim's face.

I righted myself and sat next to Tim. I had only one thought and I gave the single command that came to my mind. "Cha-cha, kill! *Kuua!*"

Cha-cha released his grip and landed in a hunched attack position. His ferocious teeth were white against his thick dark fur, his lips pulled back to show the deadly daggers and he snarled.

Bain shouted and grabbed his wrist.

"Now you are commanding wild animals to attack?" Bain yelled, not taking his eyes off of Cha-cha's stance. Cha-cha's feral growl was so low and menacing, it made the blood drain from Bain's face.

Confidence renewed, I answered Bain's question. "He is my dog, and right now he would like nothing more than to protect me from you. Now that he's got a taste of you, I'm afraid it's just a matter of time before he is chewing on your bones."

Bain reached for his knife with his right hand and positioned himself for the attack. I was grateful that Bain didn't draw his pistol, which would have been the end of Cha-cha. I could only guess that in a moment of pain and panic, Bain chose unwisely.

Cha-cha's powerful jaws clenched, his black eyes fixed on Bain. His body sank lower as all the fur on his back stood up. The growls became louder as Cha-cha began to circle Bain. Cha-cha was looking for the right moment to attack.

Like a dance, their motions mirrored one another with the same intensity, each waiting for the other to make the first move.

Tim grabbed the rifle that lay by his head and sat up. His hands shook as he lifted the gun and took aim. He hesitated.

"Do it," I encouraged. "Do it! Pull the trigger. It's the only way!"

Tim closed his eyes, Cha-cha leaped, and Bain fell when the shot rang out. Tim fell backward from the blast and he lay in the leaves, still clutching the rifle and breathing heavily.

Cha-cha stood on top of Bain, his jaw snapping only inches from Bain's face. Bain used his arm to push Cha-cha away from his face. They were two alphas struggling for dominance on the rain-soaked jungle floor.

Bain pulled his knife out of the sheath with his other hand and sunk his blade into Cha-cha's thick fur. He pulled the metal out of Cha-cha's hip. Cha-cha yelped from the pain. He began to retreat, as Bain attempted a second blow that halted when Cha-cha sprang and grabbed him by the arm. The bite made Bain yell out, and he dropped the knife.

I could see the crimson sign of Cha-cha's injury flowing slowly and soaking his fur, only to be washed away by the rain. It made it hard for me to discern the level of damage.

Bain reached for his pistol.

"No!" I screamed. "Cha-cha run. Go! *Kwenda! Kwenda!*" And I crawled toward them.

With a leap, Cha-cha released his hold and retreated to the safety of the bush. The knife lying on the ground was already washed clean of blood by the heavy rains.

Surprisingly, the shot that Tim managed to make injured Bain. The bullet grazed the top of Bain's arm. A scarlet stain crept down Bain's sleeve, slowly spreading outward. He clasped his wound and swore through his clenched teeth.

"Nothin' but trouble, the two of you. I never had so much trouble than the likes of both of you." Bain grabbed the gun from Tim and pointed it at the both of us.

"Let's go!" Bain demanded but continued to look into the bush. I assumed he was looking for Cha-cha to return.

For some reason, he changed his plan. Maybe it was the thought of Cha-cha attacking him again. Perhaps he just grew tired of the whole deadly scene. I would never know why he decided that we had to leave the area immediately.

Bain picked Tim up roughly by the arm. I supported Tim's weight and stood undefeated. But, so did Bain.

"Now, we are going to find the boss and get the hellfire outta this place. Move!"

I defiantly stood there, ready to face Bain for what he was.

"Not all the deadly animals live in the jungle, Bain."

"What's that supposed to mean?" Bain's brow pinched and he shook his head.

"It means that you are vicious and a callous killer. You have no regard for life!" I said.

"You're wrong, I care about life, just not yours. I care about *my* life, and the riches I will have. I'm not afraid to get the job done. Anything my boss wants finished gets finished. I am paid very well for my services. It's strictly business, you understand. Not that I won't enjoy killing you, Jane, just for the sheer delight."

"Killing kids doesn't make you a man!" I spat back at him.

Bain shoved me forward. "Jane, that's no way to talk to your elders. That's the problem with kids nowadays. They're not taught any manners. My boy would never think to speak to me that way. He's got manners. I am going to enjoy putting a bullet in your head for all the deceit and dishonesty."

"You have a kid? Does he know his father is a killer? Did you enjoyed killing Otis, Bain?"

"No, I am afraid I will enjoy watching you take your last breath far more. The boy, well, he is unfortunate. Just a means to an end, I'm afraid. Lots of money when we get back to the states. I'm going to be rewarded handsomely for my troubles. My son will have everything he wants with the money from killing both of you," Bain bragged.

I took a few steps, helping Tim to limp his way forward, then I stopped moving and turned toward Bain. I put my finger to my lips and tapped as if I was pondering his answer.

"When your boss dies in this jungle, where will your riches be then?" I asked. "How will you get paid when he is dead? You should have gotten your money from him up front."

"What are you talking about?" Bain's gaze shifted from me to the path that Uncle took and back to me.

I gave him a knowing grin.

Tim couldn't coordinate with my movements and he fell to the ground. The taught rope got my attention.

"Help me up."

I lifted Tim and put the wooden crutch I'd fashioned under his arm for support.

"Thank you," he whispered. His weak smile and drooping eyes told me his pain was still very much alive. Moving was going to be rough, but I had to get us moving so that I could try to rid us of Bain again.

Bain examined Tim with his scrutinizing eyes.

"Serves you right, Boy. Runnin' off like that, makin' me chase you down. You do realize that you'll never be able to outrun anything that decides to chase you, right? Maybe the creatures in this jungle will kill you before I have to trouble myself. Of course, I will take the credit so that I get paid. Now let's get to the boss and get us out of here before anything else happens."

Tim bravely put pressure on his ankle and began to sweat through his agony. Bain was right, Tim wasn't running from anything, but we had to try to move.

I darted my gaze back and forth, looking for signs. There was no sound or sign of Cha-cha, but I knew him well enough to know that he was waiting for his next chance to get to me.

"Why don't we make a deal, not that I think you can be trusted," I said.

"A deal? You are in no position to make any deal. The way I see it, I am giving you a gift by not filling you full of lead."

"And then you are stuck here and no way out. Let's say I lead you out and you agree to let us go. You can survive. You don't have to die in this jungle."

"You are going to lead me as you did before? I saw how you led the group out before. I think you tried it just to get us killed."

There must have been a flicker of truth on my face or a flush of my skin.

Bain laughed out loud. "You did exactly that! You wanted us all to die, didn'tcha, Jane? See, you and I are more alike than you think. You are just as much a killer as me."

"The name is Zura, not Jane! And no, I didn't kill anyone. The jungle did. I didn't ask you to come here. I didn't ask you to shoot my mother and kidnap me and hurt me. That's your evil-doing!" I shook with rage.

"I think I'll just call you Jane. Zura is a stupid name. No deal, Jane. No deal," he laughed with a crazed look in his eyes.

I tried to think fast. "Your boss is probably dead by now," I blurted out. "If the bacteria didn't kill him, the predators probably did. He is fat enough to feed a full-grown lion, after all. Maybe the whole pride! He probably looked like a tasty meal for something big and hungry."

Bain stared at me in disbelief. He narrowed his eyes at me and shook his head.

"No, I'm not listening to your lies any longer; he is fine. Just a little bit of stomach issues. We will get out of here and Warren will be just fine."

"I am afraid you are probably too late for that. Getting Uncle out will never happen. Especially if you kill either one of us."

I stood united with Tim. "You are wrong about your boss. He is weak and he ingested a lot of bad water, teeming with bacteria that, if untreated, will kill him. Tell me Bain, do you know what happens to the weak in Africa? Well, let me tell you. Mother Nature's alphas have a way of eliminating the weak, so that the strong may survive. Kill or be killed. Eat or be eaten. That's how it works."

Bain's eyes widened in a brief panic. I knew that he thought he had a very lucrative arrangement going, and he didn't want to lose his source of income. I also knew that he couldn't care less about his fat and lazy boss. Just his money.

"You okay?" Tim said as he wiped the blood from the cut on my forehead.

"Yeah, I am okay. Just a little dizzy. You?"

"I got you. I'll find a way to get you safe." Tim said weakly. "Come, Little Sister, let's end this journey and get you home," he whispered in my ear for encouragement.

The storm overhead had temporarily ended; the dark-gray clouds gave way to the sun's sharp rays. They pierced the canopy, allowing sunbeams to pour between the openings in the trees. The ray's painted pale yellow hues on the watery leaves.

Something on the ground caught the light and glistened. The brightness lying near Cha-cha's escape route was exactly what I needed. It was a stroke of luck.

My forehead burned from the blow I took, but my eyes stopped swirling. I could see the path we needed to follow. It led to that shiny object that caught my attention.

I carefully avoided drawing attention to my target. The knife that pierced Cha-cha's hip lay on the ground, bending the light that shown on its blade.

I pretended to trip as we approached the knife and folded it under my body. It slid easily into the pocket of my shorts, and I covered it with my shirt.

Tim and I shared a glance. Whoever said that children were weak or couldn't do things that grownups could do was deadly wrong. I felt as though Tim and I could do anything as we drew closer to Thinking Rock.

Bain interrupted my thoughts. "Let's go see where the boss went. Move!" He shoved his heavy-footed boot into my back and propelled me forward.

I helped Tim along the way by supporting his weight. I became his second crutch, not caring how much it hurt me. I would have time for pain later.

We didn't have to go far into the bush before we came upon Uncle's body. He laid on the ground, his pants still around his ankles. It was unsightly to see what damage the bacteria had done to his intestines and what destruction happened to him either before or after he was already dead. His throat was wide open, exposing whatever lives within the neck. His face was purple as if his windpipe was cut off from receiving air. The bite was distinct. It wasn't a lion attack or another large cat. They do far more damage and don't just kill; they kill to eat. And no portion of Uncle's body had been eaten. It was canine; a dog bite.

His leg had another vicious bite just below the knee. My best guess was that is how he brought Uncle down. Uncle's eyes were affixed in a dead stare toward the sky. Even in death, he appeared miserable and mean-spirited. The amount of blood on the front of his shirt told the story of his death. He suffered a great deal, I was sure of it.

Bain bent down to check for a pulse in Uncle's neck.

"He's dead," Bain said in disbelief.

"Of course he is dead," Tim said without emotion. I could have sworn that relief shown on his youthful face.

I stepped over Uncle's dead body and I stared into Bain's evil, hard-set eyes. "You shouldn't have messed with my dog," I said, emotionless. "He doesn't like people hurting me and will protect me to the death."

"Your dog? You are insane, Jane. That was a wild animal." Bain stood on wobbly legs. His boss's dead body and the loss of his promised riches shook him to the core.

I grinned at Bain's misfortune. "Yes, he is. He's wild and magnificent and he is mine. Cha-cha probably has it out for you, so if I were you, I wouldn't spend much more time in this jungle. Cha-cha will kill anything or anyone that hurts me. And the way I see it, you have done too much damage for him to forgive you."

"*Forgive me*? We are talking about a dog, right?"

"Mess with me again and then ask him how he feels about it before he kills you. The name is Zura!" I said, maybe a little too cocky. I walked away from the conversation triumphant and renewed. I looked one last time at Uncle's dead body.

"Let's leave him like he left the rest of the people he got killed." I tapped my finger against my lips. "Let me see, how did Uncle word it? Oh yeah, *he's part of the jungle now*." I served my words dripping with sarcasm. "You'll be next, Bain. Cha-cha already got a taste of your arm and it will be *your* throat next time."

Bain seemed stunned into silence with the death of Uncle. He certainly had to decide whether to kill me and stay in the jungle, unable to find his way out, or trust me to lead him out so that he could get back to the United States.

"Okay, Jane. I'll take you up on your offer. You get me out, and you and the boy get to live. But I will not be returning with the boy. He stays here."

I turned and eyed him for a few seconds. "Deal," I answered and turned around to keep walking.

Tim looked nervous and he pulled on the rope. "You know you can't rely on him to keep that promise. Don't you, Zura?"

I pulled back on the rope. "I don't trust anything that comes out of Bain's mouth," I whispered. "Nothing has changed. I just have to find a way for us to escape again."

"He won't take his eyes off us. He trusts us just about as much as we trust him."

"But he needs us. We don't need him. That puts us on top."

"On top of what?" Tim eyed me as if I had lost my mind.

"I don't know, just on top."

CHAPTER 8

I was dirty, tired and in pain but kept moving us forward. Still not knowing where to lead us, I steered the three of us back and around to the other side of the mountain.

The rains subsided temporarily, but I could feel a brewing storm in the air. The ground was soggy. Our feet were sinking into the muddy earth, which made it more difficult to travel.

Tim was starting to move better and he said the pain was lessening. It was a good sign.

Bain felt the need to remind me where we were going. He was able to tell me the location, and I knew where we were supposed to go. But it was not where I was going to take us. I thought if Bain saw new parts of the jungle, he wouldn't realize I was leading him closer to my home.

A fresh clean stream sliced through the foliage, it's flow constant and heading toward its purpose. It was a perfect spot to rest. The tiny fish nervously darted when I took off my muddy boots and placed my tired feet into the water. It felt glorious standing there with the little pebbles and sand squishing between my toes.

"Tim get your ankle into the water. It will help the swelling," I said, leaning down to wash some of the dirt off my arms and legs. Tim did as I instructed, and he sighed with relief.

"Bain, Tim needs to rest," I said.

Bain only grunted, and I took that as his reluctant agreement.

I built a small fire. Bain lit it and placed a small kettle on the hot wood. He pulled three metal cups from his gear and I boiled water for some tea. The leaves from my pocket were soggy from the rain, but the hot liquid renewed my energy as I sipped it slowly, letting the liquid heat my throat and belly.

Bain tended to his wounded useless left arm, compliments of his encounter with Cha-cha and the graze of the bullet on his left shoulder from Tim's attempt to shoot him. He grumbled the whole time about it not being the worst injury he has had. He said something about the war and how he killed more men than those who tried to kill him.

"Alright, enough rest." Bain became increasingly impatient with the setting of the sun. "Enough downtime, let's see if we can do another half mile before dark." He kicked some dirt over the fire to smother the heat.

We barely made it another quarter of a mile before Tim's other leg became unsteady from trying to brace his steps and maneuvering around rocks and tree limbs on the uneven jungle floor. He fell several times before Bain allowed us to stop and rest for the night.

The jungle came alive at night. Insects chirped in harmony, creating different pitches of songs. Frogs croaked as they hunted for unsuspecting victims. The stars sprinkled the night sky and the moon shone full and brilliant.

Bain built a fire to last the night and used another rope to tie Tim's wrist to Bain's leg. "If you get any notions about escaping, I am going to know about it." Bain glared at me through the fire. "I'll kill him if you so much as pull too hard."

I piled leaves to make a comfortable bed for Tim and me. Tim sighed as I propped his swollen ankle on a rock to keep it elevated.

I laid beside Tim, feeling protective and responsible for his safety during the night. I could see the eerily glowing reflection of a pair of eyes shining through the trees. They were still and silent in the darkened foliage. If I were to guess, I would say it was Cha-cha, waiting for a chance to get to me. I could not stand the fact that he may put himself in danger again to try to save me. And not knowing the extent of his injuries worried me.

When I heard the exhausted snoring coming from Bain on the other side of the fire, I knew it was time to think quickly of a plan. I raised my hand and gave the signal to stay. I wanted to tell Cha-cha to guard so that he knew not to attack. "Cha-cha, *askari*," I whispered into the dark trees, hoping it was him and not some other creature waiting to strike when we fell asleep. I would have preferred a bed in the trees where I knew it was much safer. There was safety in numbers. I wasn't too concerned when there was so many of us, like a herd, but with just the three of us, we were fair game to any predator wandering too close to our location.

Bain let out a loud snore and began to stir. He must have woken himself up, but he continued to rest his head on his backpack, the rifle laid across his chest. He kept his eyes closed when he spoke. "Jane, don't be talkin' that jungle language."

"I speak Swahili. I am proud to know it." I countered, grabbing Tim's hand for support for both of us.

"Well, know it some other time. Wish I thought to grab my knife, never know when I might need it," Bain mumbled. I remembered that the knife was in my pocket.

Tim suddenly sat up. "Bain, I would like to make you a new deal."

Bain's laugh was deep, dripping in mockery. "You are in no position to be makin' deals, the way I see it. You should be begging for your life. You and that filthy, deceitful, jungle girl."

"I will not beg," Tim countered. "You forgot about the only thing that you care about besides yourself."

"And what might that be? It certainly ain't you brats. The only care I have now is to get home in one piece to my boy. He is a way smarter kid than the both of you. There is noth…"

"The money," Tim said with confidence. "You forgot about the money."

"There's no… you…" Bain froze and his eyes became wide when the knowledge hit him over the head.

"That's right," Tim smiled. "You figured it out? I have all the money now that Uncle is dead. I am his only living relative. I can make you very rich. This trip doesn't have to end this way. You can have it all. For you and your boy to live in luxury for the rest of both your lives."

"I'm listening," Bain said, sitting up and throwing another limb on the fire. It sent smoke into the air from its wet leaves. Bain coughed as it blew in his direction. "I hate this jungle. Didn't want to come here anyway," he muttered.

Tim beamed with a confidence that I had not witnessed since I met him. "If you take us to Zura's home, get her there safely, and not hurt her in any way, I will get my ankle fixed up, and we can get back to the States. We can get a truck from there and get to a plane. I will pay you whatever you think Uncle owes you and you walk away. But I never want to see your scary face again."

"Who is Zura?"

"I am Zura," I interrupted, "That's my name. I told you before. Now that you know it, never call me Jane again. It's not my name," I said, glaring at Bain.

"Sounds like a dumb name to me. What's it even mean?"

"What does it matter what my name means?"

"It doesn't. It's a stupid name. I couldn't care less if it means sunbeam and rainbows, or whatever your stupid dead mother wanted to call you," Bain said and turned his attention back to Tim.

"Let's just suppose that we get her back to her home, how do I know that you won't report me to someone? I did, after all, kill Otis. And you brats know it."

"Reporting you won't get me home. I would never be able to negotiate my way back to the States by myself. Who is going to believe a kid?"

Bain scratched his chin and pondered Tim's words. He eyed Tim suspiciously.

"How do I know you'll keep your word? You ain't tryin' to trick me, Boy, are you?"

"I just want to get Zura home safe. She is all that matters to me now. I owe her that. I want to leave this jungle and never see it again."

Tim and I shared a look. His eyes were somber, so I believed that he might want to leave me when this was all over. It hurt. I became used to him and wanted him to stay and grow up with me. I knew we could never trust Bain and his word and Tim's deal worried me.

"No, Tim, you can't trust that he will follow through with anything he says. Remember, he hates us. A man that would shoot Otis without a single second thought is a cold-blooded killer. We can't trust him."

"Zura, I know what I'm doing. Trust me. I said I would get you home, and this is the only way now. I can barely walk. If you had a mirror and could see how beat up you are, you would know why I am concerned about you, Little Sister."

Bain forced out a loud laugh. "She ain't your sister! You don't have a sister. In fact, you don't have anybody," Bain said sadistically. "And, since we found this brat in this here jungle, you've done nothin' but lie and deceive any chance you got. Nothing you have done tells me you would follow through with our deal. In fact, I bet you are planning to squeal the first chance you get. I am not spending the rest of my life in a jungle jail, or a Chicago jail, or any other jail for that matter. The two of you are the only witnesses alive, and I'll be damned if I let either one of you send me to prison. No deal! Now, get some sleep. I don't want to hear another word about some stinking deal. We are getting out of this jungle at first light, right Jaaane?" He taunted me. "Go to sleep!"

Bain threw some more wood on the fire and laid back down and hugged his rifle. His snoring came quickly for the second time.

My mind would not let me sleep. I knew I would not be so lucky to find another opportunity to escape with Tim's slow pace. Thinking Rock wasn't far away, and I knew that if we could make it to its base, we might have a chance. Saving the two of us was all I could afford to have on my mind. Well, and Cha-cha, if that was him waiting in the bushes.

I lie awake, unable to sleep for fear of what might be hunting us. I had to hope it was Cha-cha and not something much more dangerous. When I heard Bain's snoring grow louder, I knew it was safe to release our bonds. I took the knife from my pocket and cut the line that tied Tim to Bain then I cut the rope that bonded Tim and me.

A bittersweet moment. I knew if I wanted to, I could slip into the trees and disappear from their sight forever. Tim would surely die if I left him there to fend for himself, either at the hands of Bain or any predator that came upon him. I knew I couldn't live with myself if I abandoned the boy who literally had no one else in the world but me. He knew it too, yet he whispered for me to go. "Zura, run. Get yourself home."

"Never. Not without you." I stood firm on my final decision. "Ssh," I cautioned and placed my finger to my lips. Tim nodded, and I slid into the trees and circled quickly to the other side of the fire, where Bain slept. He was on his back, using his backpack as a pillow. His hands were folded across his stomach, still holding the gun. Bain's ankles were crossed with his feet close to the fire.

I held the knife in both of my shaking hands. I was prepared to stab Bain in the heart. His death would be quicker if I thrust the metal blade swiftly and rapidly. As I made up my mind to *kill instead of being killed*, I realized the decision was harder than I thought it would be. I looked over at Tim for encouragement and he motioned for me to do it.

My movements came down, just as Bain's hand came up and he shifted. He grabbed my hands over the handle of the knife and tried to stop my momentum. But he could only use his right arm, so it weakened his ability to ward off my attack. The blade sank deeply into his shoulder. I had missed my mark.

He pushed me backward, the knife falling with me. Bain grabbed his shoulder and bellowed in pain. "You little bitch!" He swore and tried to sit up.

I searched the leaves for anything that could help me, anything that could give me an edge over Bain's strength. My search turned up a good size rock and I didn't hesitate. I hit him firmly on the head. Bain slumped back down. I wasn't sure if the blow was enough to kill him, but I doubted it.

I circled the fire, lit a limb for light and helped Tim to his feet. I grabbed Bain's backpack in hopes of finding supplies. We tried to move quickly. I secured the backpack on Tim's shoulders. "You carry this, and I'll carry you," I said.

"No way! I'll hurt your shoulder."

"It barely even hurts anymore," I lied. "Come on, Tim! We don't have time to argue. If I can't carry you, we will think of something else. Now get on!"

Tim caved to my wishes and he got on my back. I wrapped my arms around his legs. He held the burning limb in front of us, and we quickened our pace. My injuries paled to what would happen to me if Bain woke and tracked us, so I pushed through the pain.

"The gun!" Tim yelled. "We should have taken the rifle and the pistol. Why didn't I think of that?"

"Because we never did this before, because we were in a hurry and because we are stupid kids," I said, angry with myself for not even thinking of the guns.

I was out of breath and had to put Tim down after about half a mile. I knew it was not nearly enough space between us if Bain decided to follow. "Just give me a minute," I said through my heavy breath.

A rustling sound came from the bushes. I grabbed the knife. "Stay behind me." I was shaking with fear.

Cha-cha limped toward me and whimpered. He wobbled, but still wanted to protect me. Cha-cha snarled at Tim, bearing his dagger-sharp teeth, and tried to nip at Tim's boot.

I tried to console Cha-cha as best I could. "It's alright boy, Tim is a friend. He's not hurting me."

As if he understood, Cha-cha's whimpering and snapping jaws stopped.

"Get on," I said to Tim. "We have to get as much distance as possible. Let's get going."

I carried Tim for another half hour or so before my arms burned and my back felt like it was going to break. We stopped at the stream near the waterfall and Thinking Rock.

Eyes shone on the other side of the water. Antelope huddled together for protection. In the trees, the gray parrots perched, not ready to start their loud calls until the sun came up. An aardwolf was eating termites from a large mound. He looked like a cross between Cha-cha, with his big ears, and his larger cousin, the hyena. He was wary of us but continued his nocturnal meal.

As the sun rose and a gentle mist hovered over the stream, the morning sky slowly changed from darkness to hues of orange and pink. But dark storm clouds were blowing in, heavy with rain, and beginning to cover the sky.

"Why is it always raining here?" Tim whispered as I placed him down to sit on a rock.

"Not all the time, but this is an extremely wet season."

"Zura, I think I can walk now," Tim said. "I at least want to try.

"Alright, we can try. Let me check Cha-cha, I said, leaning down to pet the top of Cha-cha's head.

Tim tried to sit as far away from Cha-cha as he could.

I sat down beside Cha-cha to check his wound. Because I had more light, I could see that Cha-cha had blood on his muzzle, chest and back. I opened his mouth and looked for where he was hurt. The blood was in his fur and all over my hands by the time I was done combing his body, looking for injuries. I didn't care about how bad the blood looked on me. I only cared that I took care of my faithful dog. I couldn't bear to lose Cha-cha.

"Oh, Tim look at him. Something else must have attacked him. He is bloody everywhere. It's dripping off his muzzle, but I can't see the wound."

"Pour water on him," Tim said, searching Bain's backpack. He pulled out a canteen and I filled it with water from the stream. I cleaned the wound first and could see the puncture from Bain's knife. I worked my way up, soaking his thick fur and rubbing it, searching for teeth marks or torn flesh. I made my way to the worst of it, Cha-cha's muzzle. Washing most of the blood off him, I realized what I was seeing.

Terror sickened me as I comprehended that Cha-cha's only injury was his punctured hip. It barely oozed. Most of the wound's blood was old and dried. The blood I was rubbing was not Cha-cha's blood. And I looked down at my crimson-covered hands. It was Bain's blood. I had his blood all over. I literally had his death on my hands.

Cha-cha, my fierce protector. The most loyal of wild dogs had drunk the blood of my enemy.

The thought of Cha-cha bringing down Bain and drinking his blood made me nauseous. I leaned to the side and threw up in the bushes. The bile burned my throat and made me cough.

"What's wrong with him? What's wrong with you? Are you

sick?" Tim questioned. He eyed Cha-cha suspiciously. "You didn't drink the bad water, did you, Zura? That's a lot of blood. Where is the wound?" Tim did not try to move closer. He kept his distance. "That's not from his hip, is it? It doesn't look that serious of a wound to bleed like that."

"It's not his blood," I whispered. "It's Bain's blood. Now Bain's blood is all over me. He must have drank it or something. Maybe he tried to eat him." I quickly rubbed my blood-soaked hands in the water to remove the traces of Bain's blood.

The knowledge showed clearly on Tim's horrified face. "You think he must have killed Bain? He might have eaten him?" Tim paled.

"I think so, yes. To protect us."

Tim lifted his head defiantly and looked off into the rising sun. "I knew since before this trip what the plans were for me. They brought me here to kill me. I heard Uncle and Bain's conversation with Bain one day when they thought I was in another room. Uncle was telling Bain that there would be an extra bonus in his pay if he saw to it that I became *lost or dead* in the jungle. My life was worth a lot of money. Can you imagine how much he has if he was willing to pay so much for my death? Filthy rich. It's really hard. Knowing that someone would rather have you dead than take you in and love you. Especially when it's family. I don't understand him and I guess I never will."

"It must hurt you to know your uncle didn't want you."

"Yeah, he told me I would be going to boarding school when we got back. But I knew it was a lie. He wanted me dead. Now *he* is dead. Ironic, isn't it?"

"Tim, we will sort it all out. My father and mo...." The words died on my tongue. I could only swallow down the lump in my throat. Not knowing whether my mother was dead or alive, I just had to believe that she would be alright. I knew Tim was missing his as well.

Tim grabbed my filthy hand with his own. "My brave Little Sister, we have come so far. Let's get you home." He rose. "Should I try to just limp on my leg and at least carry your dog?" He said, bending down to place a hand on Cha-cha's neck.

"Don't!" I said. "He doesn't let anyone else touch him but me."

As the words left my lips, Cha-cha was completely still. Tim cautiously rubbed him behind the ear. Cha-cha closed his eyes in delight. There was no growling, no attack. Cha-cha melted into the rubbing by Tim. He lowered his head and closed his eyes, clearly enjoying the attention. I never saw him look so content, not even from my touch. Dogs sensed people's energy and Cha-cha must have known Tim's kind and gentle way. Tim carefully lifted Cha-cha, who rested his head on Tim's arm. "His fur is softer than I thought."

We shared a smile. "A boy and his dog," I teased.

"Yeah, I always wanted a dog," Tim said. He continued to limp, but somehow taking care of Cha-cha, took his mind off his ankle. He was still in pain, but he slowly made his way.

"I was never allowed to have one. My father hated animals in the house, and my mother hated them outside the house. They could never agree. I always asked for a big dog, not some little ankle biter. You know, one like Cha-cha's size," Tim said with a smile that looked good on him. "But I think he is too big for me to carry," he said, gently putting Cha-cha down. "I'm sorry, I don't think I can carry him. I feel bad."

It's alright, Tim, Cha-cha will follow. We are all in pain, so we will all support each other." My brain was always working, always figuring out what to do next. "I have an idea," I said.

"What are you thinking?"

"You have to trust me on this, okay?"

"I don't like the sound of that. Usually, when people say that you have to trust them, it turns out bad."

"Not this time, I promise."

As we moved slowly through the dense foliage, I made sure to keep my eyes peeled for any dangerous creature. I could hear the call of the elephants in the distance and it made my heart leap. Somewhere ahead of our trail, there was a herd. Not just any herd but, probably my mother's favorite herd. The one that included my Tembo might be very close to our location.

It took several minutes to reach the end of the stream at the base of the waterfall. A dreamy white fog lay lazily on the tops of the trees above the waterfall, adding to its mystery and magic. Water cascaded forcefully over the rocks. The current at the base of the waterfall was rushing and pounding, a welcoming sound to hear. It meant home was close by; just a few more hours and we would be safe at last.

Tim pet Cha-cha's head. "There you go, boy. Are you feeling better?" Tim asked a panting Cha-cha. He helped his new friend to the water for a drink. Cha-cha lapped until he had his fill.

I knew that this particular water was clean. I'd drunk from it before, so I didn't hesitate to enjoy the fresh cool sips. I splashed the freshening water on my face and neck, scrubbing to remove the dirt and sweat from some of me. The liquid made my body feel prickly and refreshed and cooled my overheated skin.

"Watch for crocodiles. They hide very well."

Tim puddled water quickly in his hands and rubbed it on Cha-cha's back to cool him off. He was careful to stay away from the puncture on his leg. The entire time, he searched the water for danger.

A whisper of a sound caught my attention, and the smell of cigar filled my nose. He had a heavy gate. Bain never moved gracefully. Bain stomped like a hippo, plodding wherever he decided to travel, so he made a lot of noise. He was close and getting closer by the second. The blow to his head with the rock did not kill him and Cha-cha didn't try to eat him after all. I knew that we had to move—and fast.

"We have to go!"

Tim picked up on the panic in my voice. "What's wrong?"

"Bain. He's alive and coming this way. I think he is tracking us. We have to get moving!"

Tim picked up Cha-cha and looked at me worriedly. "I thought the dog tried to eat him. Where do we go?"

"Nope, I would know that smell anywhere. We go up," I pointed toward the sky.

"Up? What do you mean *up*?"

He followed my eyes as they gravitated toward the waterfall and Tim shook his head. "Up there? You want us to climb all the way up there?"

"Not entirely. There's no time to argue, just follow me."

I knew that Tim would never agree to my plan, so I held back what I was planning until I had to make my drastic move. I took Cha-cha because I was a better climber. I wore my dog around the back of my neck and held his feet with one hand while I used the other to balance. We began to climb a hidden ledge on the right side of the falls. I knew it well because I had discovered it on one of my many explorations. Other than some bats, I knew it to be safe. There was a second entrance on the other side of the cliff, but it was too far for us to waste time. We had to get high and hidden.

"Tim, we have to get behind the waterfall," I said.

"I don't understand. Behind the falls?"

"Yes. There is a cave. Bain will never find us there. No one knows about it."

"Then how do you know about it?" Tim questioned.

"Because I am Zura, child of the jungle, that's why."

"Well, how do we get there?"

"We climb."

What had started as a soft rain continued to grow in intensity. It made our journey extremely dangerous on the slippery rocks. Tim climbed in front of me and I inched my way while balancing a heavy Cha-cha. The ledge opened up to a cave. The dark damp cave chilled me. The sound of the falls was deafening, but the blanket of water concealed us from danger. I opened the backpack and found a flashlight and handed it to Tim.

The beam traced the etchings on the walls and I heard him gasp as he shined the light on the cave's ceiling.

A moving river of tiny black bodies with beady eyes shown in the filtered light. Tim gasped and blindly shined the light brightly into my eyes. "Did you see that? We have to get out of here before they attack us."

"I can't see anything with you blinding me with that light. They are just harmless bats. They won't hurt us."

"Are you sure? They look like the devil. Look at their beady eyes. Do they have fangs? I read in a book once that they drink your blood." Tim's eyes widened, and his pupils were the size of a river pebble.

"That's baloney. The bats won't get you. Cha-cha would eat them first. He may be hurt, but he will never stop protecting us. It's in his blood." I scrubbed the top of Cha-cha's head. "Right boy?" I said as he leaned his body into Tim. He just did the unthinkable, and I felt a little jealous. He claimed Tim. That lean told me exactly what I needed to know. Cha-cha would protect Tim.

I was as ready as I could be for what I had to do. "I need you to make sure that Cha-cha stays still and hidden until I can get help. My home isn't too far, and I will get help. My father should be back from his trip. I'll bring him and his men to help us."

"No, Zura. It's too dangerous, even for you. Bain is still out there," Tim pleaded.

"He will not catch me."

"You are not faster than his bullets. You know that."

I could not let Tim know that I was scared or he would never let me go alone. "Trust me. I am like a lioness, and I will get there safely. Stay hidden. Stay here." I rubbed Cha-cha behind his ear. "Keep him safe."

"I will," said Tim.

"I was talking to our dog," I said and smiled at Tim.

He smiled back. "Be careful. I don't want to lose my sister now that I found you."

I kissed his cheek. "Don't worry, Brother. I am a child of this jungle, remember?"

"How can I forget? You tell me all the time," Tim teased.

We stared at each other for a moment and I turned to go. I did not look back, unsure if I would ever see the two of them again.

CHAPTER 9

The rains came hard and steady. I followed the path around the cliff and down the side of the waterfall. The ground was soggy and the mud under my boots made them feel heavier and heavier, like I was laboring in quicksand, pulling me down. I refused to fall victim to Bain and his quest for my death. No longer driven by money, he was even more of a threat. He wanted revenge.

I focused intently on the vibrations of the jungle, letting her tell me where danger might be lurking. There was just one more person to eliminate and then we would be free. No child should ever have to think that way. But life in this land was harsh, and the weak never survived, so I had to remain strong.

I carefully crossed the lower part of the river. As I reached the other side, Bain came out of the trees and into my line of vision. We locked eyes from across the river as he raised his rifle. I didn't waste time waiting for him to find me in his sights. I ran like the cheetah, closer and closer to Thinking Rock, where I knew I had a chance to beat him. I could hear him splashing as he crossed the water, running after me. He was yelling obscenities at me, but I just kept going.

"Jane, I'm going to rip your beating heart clean out of your chest!"

I raced to the bottom of Thinking Rock. Out of breath and soaked from the rain, I looked up and chose my path. Without even thinking, I began to scale its slick surface. I picked the fastest route and planted my feet firmly with each step, knowing the surface almost as well as my own rapid heartbeat. I stopped on a ledge about halfway from the top. When I looked over the side, Bain was finding his footing close to the bottom.

"I'll get you this time Jaaane! When I catch you, I'll throw your dead carcass off the top of this cliff! There is nowhere for you to run."

He was right. There was nowhere else for me to run. I could only pray for a miracle.

If only one of the eagles that sometimes visited Thinking Rock would swoop down and scoop me up in their talons and deliver me home. I couldn't spare the brain power for such daydreaming; I had to stay focused so I pushed the eagle rescue thoughts from my mind, and looked over the side of the mountain for Bain. There was no sign of him; at least, I could not get a glimpse of him, so I continued my quest to the top.

I climbed higher and higher. I was not afraid of the familiar height and I continued to climb the rain-soaked rocks, for it was my refuge, my escape. With the stealth of the lioness and the speed of the cheetah, I scaled the slippery path, moving up and out of the way of danger. I had climbed the path a thousand times, but never to escape, never with the fear that I may not live through the day. I could only hope that he could not follow where I went with ease.

When I made it to the top I was breathing heavy and my heart pumped fast and hard in my chest. Never had I ever climbed at such a reckless pace before. My usual purposeful climbs were for enjoyment, not survival.

From the view on the top of the cliff, I could see the mist as it danced over the treetops. I could see the force of the waterfall as the water rushed over the rocks. It cascaded down to the welcoming river below and fed the wildlife that rested by its banks. I contemplated whether I should jump, but I was up too high and knew that I could never survive the fall.

Yes, Bain was right. I had nowhere else to go. I could no longer run from him. It would be Thinking Rock where I needed to make my stand.

Still, there was no sign of my enemy, only the animals that looked small from my high observation.

Crocodiles and hippos, even the giraffe was dwarfed from that height. They were oblivious to the dangers that faced me. I couldn't help but wish that one of the crocks would make a meal of Bain and I would be free.

I shivered from the wet rain that pelted my body, but mostly I trembled out of fear for who hunted me.

Bain was near. I couldn't see him, but I felt the presence of his evil.

Suddenly, he appeared behind me. I could hear his labored breath as it came in gasps. I turned slowly. From where he stood, I could tell that he had circled the cliff and used the path that Cha-cha used when we would race each other to the top. I wasn't sure why I hadn't thought to use the easier path. I knew that I wasn't thinking clearly and that I had scaled the cliff out of memory and nothing else.

Bain pointed the rifle at me, and I backed away. His eyes were wild and crazy, like he had mentally gone over the edge. The rain diluted the blood from the cut on his head where I had hit him with the rock and the liquid smeared down his face.

"Well, Jaaane, it's just you and me? Tell me, where is the boy?"

I didn't hesitate with my answer. "Tim's dead. A lion attacked us, and Tim couldn't run away. He's part of the jungle now." I looked him in the eye and stared intently.

"So, you got another one dead, is that right? Another victim to the jungle girl." He let out a vile laugh. "The only one that you wanted to survive, you got him killed too. If only you would have warned the boss about the water, and Jasper about the snake. I bet you knew that we were being stalked by that lion that killed Clint, am I right?"

He found my weakness; shame. I did nothing, I said nothing, just watched people die.

Bain aimed his gun at me, but I didn't look away. I looked down the barrel of his gun and held my breath.

I saw a blur of gray, black and tan. Cha-cha had followed me from the cave and used the same path that Bain had used to get to the top. Cha-cha jumped on top of Bain, biting him on the shoulder and neck. It was a vicious attack that caused Bain to pull the trigger. A sharp burning pain sliced my thigh. And I lost my footing and tumbled off the side of the cliff, hitting sharp rocks that protruded from the base. Cutting, slicing, the jagged rocks gouged my flesh. And as fast as it all started, it stopped. The fall had ended.

I lay there waiting for death to take me, waiting to feel some sort of peace as my soul slipped from my broken body, but I felt nothing. I was beaten, shattered, and defeated.

It was hard to breathe. The impact had taken the air from my lungs. And they burned, burned like the fires of hell.

I rolled to my side and realized I was lying on the edge of an overhang, suspended by the slightest ledge. It held me tight, like a mother to its child. But one wrong move and I would fall to the dangerous depth and to my death. I pinned myself against the wall and waited to regain my vision and breath. My body shook, and I took stock of my appendages. I was severely bruised all over and ached. My thigh had caught Bain's shot and now the wound burned. It had only grazed the top of my leg but was painful. I knew I had to stop the bleeding somehow, but I was afraid to move until my vision cleared completely. I could hear only silence coming from the cliff above me and had to assume the worst. That Cha-cha was dead. If that were true, it meant that Bain was close, maybe too close. I knew that danger couldn't be far away. Bain had to know where to find me. I closed my eyes and waited for Bain to finish me off. But he did not come for me on that ledge.

Time ticked by; maybe an hour passed before I heard him. Bain had climbed back down. I listened to him below me screaming my name as insanity took hold of him.

"Jane! Where are you? Jaaane! I'll find your dead body, and still, I'll fill you full of lead! I hope you're dead!" The screaming continued as if he couldn't stop. "And when I am done with you, I'll find that wild mutt of yours and skin him alive!"

Cha-cha was alive! That renewed my hope that I could live too. I cautiously lifted my head. I saw the herd of elephants from my perch as they approached Bain's location. They were startled and angered by his noise. They froze their postures to determine if Bain was a threat.

The elephant's sounds rumbled low, sending a vibration through the air. As I saw them approach Bain, I needed to make a decision to climb up to look for Cha-cha or climb down towards the herd. I knew Cha-cha would be able to hide, or he may have gone down to ready himself to attack Bain again. I carefully began to climb down as fast as my tired and sore body could manage. All the while, Bain continued his tirade, which offended the very soul of the jungle. He disrupted the flow of things and made himself a target.

Bain was too distracted by the sound of his insanity to hear the approaching herd. It was my chance to get down even further, maybe to lose him in the trees.

I continued to climb down the side of the cliff until the trees were within my reach. I pushed through the pain in my shoulder and thigh and kept moving as quietly as I could.

There was a perfect tree with low branches in front of me. The leaves were broad, so I knew they would shelter me. Putting my right arm on the lowest branch, I hoisted myself and wrapped my good leg around the limb. Continuing the painful process over and over, I soon found myself hidden well in the wet leaves. I funneled a few of the leaves and let the rainwater drip into my mouth, soothing my dry-cracked lips. I took a few moments to renew.

Bain was in my sight. He was completely unaware of exactly how much danger waited for him with the herd.

There, on the other side of the trees, stood Tembo in all of his brilliance. He spread his ears wide and took on an aggressive stance. His head held high and his tusks lifted toward the sky, he was beautiful. His eyes locked on Bain.

Tembo's large body crashed through the trees with a loud uprooting. He swung his head and stomped the ground, in a wondrous show of aggression. My heart renewed with hope. Hope for me. Hope for Tim and Cha-cha. Hope that I would shortly be reunited with my family. I grew impatient.

"Tembo, come here!" I yelled "Tembo, *kuja hapa, kuja hapa,* Tembo!"

He turned his magnificent head toward me and knew my voice. His misshaped ear perked in my direction, and I could swear he smiled.

Bain raised his rifle and screamed at a very agitated and aggressive, Tembo.

I clamped my eyes tight, not wanting to see the slaughter. "No! Tembo!"

When I opened my watery eyes again, I saw the dangerous beauty of an angry elephant.

The shot never rang out. Bain never had the chance to pull the trigger. With a loud trumpet of anger, Tembo charged Bain, piercing him with his mighty tusks and tossing him aside. With a grunt, Tembo trampled Bain's already dead body, and smashed it into the ground before crushing his skull under the weight of his enormous foot. Bain was the last of the men to become part of the jungle forever.

The trumpeting music of the elephants' voices was a welcoming sound. I tightly tied the sling around my leg to stop the bleeding and I made my way down the tree.

I sat there impatiently waiting for my life-long friend. There he was, not as I remembered. He was more. I believed there was never a more beautiful creature put on this earth. And he never forgot me as I thought he would. My hero, my friend.

Tembo made a low growling sound. It was his hello. He rubbed his trunk on the top of my head, and I let the tears flow. I hurt all over. I believed he knew the extent of my pain and injuries. He lifted his mighty trunk, and let out a sound that rumbled my belly as he brushed my cheek. I knew he didn't have human emotions but I couldn't help but think he tried to comfort me in his own way. Elephants are smart.

"Tembo, *chini,*" I said. "*Chini.*"

He remembered my command from our early years, and bent at the knees to lay beside me. I grabbed hold of him and painfully pulled myself up onto his back. I leaned forward to lay my head on his. Using a light touch on either ear, I was able to guide him toward Tim.

Remarkably, the herd followed him. Usually, bull elephants leave the herd, but not Tembo. His family. Supporting one another. It reminded me of Tim and Cha-cha. I had to get to them and support them.

I led Tembo to the waterfall and he stopped to take a drink at its banks. There was no way for me to climb back up to get Tim and had to trust that he could safely make his way back down. "Tim!" I yelled. "Tim! Climb down. It's alright. We can go home now, I said with tears streaming down my cheeks. I hugged Tembo, so grateful for him. It was strange to feel his wrinkled skin under my hands for the first time in a very long time.

Tim's answer was muffled by the sound of the falls. I hoped that he understood my message.

It wasn't long before I saw him with a renewed confidence.

He stared at Tembo and me, his mouth agape. Tim took his time climbing down, but he made it to the bottom. As he turned to see the herd, his face paled. "Cha-cha, he was there one minute, and he took off the next. I didn't have time to grab him before he left me all alone in the cave." Tim eyed Tembo suspiciously. "What in heaven? You really are the Jungle Girl!"

I laughed, and Tim relaxed a bit. "Tembo, *chini*," I repeated my instruction, and Tembo kneeled.

Tim eyed Tembo and me suspiciously. "Why is your sling tied around your leg and why is it bloody?"

"Bain shot at me. It's okay, Tim. Let's just get home. We can deal with it when we get there. If you stall much longer, I may bleed out, so get on."

"Get on? Get on what?"

"Tembo. Stop stalling. Let's go," I demanded. "You will have to hand Cha-cha up to me. He can sit up front. You can sit behind me and hold on. Alright?"

"Sure, but where is Cha-cha?" Tim questioned cautiously.

Cha-cha appeared out of the tree line. He hobbled over to us. "Where did you go?" Tim pet the top of Cha-cha's head. "He has blood on his face again. Why does this dog always have blood on his face?"

"He attacked Bain."

"I see. Did he drink his blood? He is covered again."

"No. I fell over the edge and landed on a ledge, but Bain climbed the whole way down looking for me. I guess Cha-cha attacked and then retreated."

Tim looked horrified by my tale of what happened, so I saved the rest of the story.

"Let's go! Hand Cha-cha up to me."

Tim carefully handed Cha-cha up and then he grabbed the fabric of my shirt to pull himself up. He flung his injured ankle over Tembo's back and sat up straight behind me.

"Move with him," I coached Tim. Just adjust your weight to his movements, and you won't fall off."

Tembo shifted as he stood, and Tim held on to me tightly. "Is this right?" Tim questioned.

"Yep, you did a perfectly good job."

I pet Cha-cha's fur, and he seemed to relax. "Good boy, Cha-cha," I crooned. "You took great care of Tim and me. Good boy. You helped to save my life. More than once."

We traveled the few miles to home but our pace was slow and the journey stretched on for hours. I couldn't help but wonder whether part of Bain was still on the bottom of Tembo's mighty foot. Are we dragging parts of him back to the sanctuary, back to my shelter from his evil? My mind continued to replay the stomping of his head and the crushing sound of his skull under Tembo's weight. That sickening breaking noise and the sudden silence of Bain screaming my name. The view of his lifeless, mangled body. And the smell of blood soaking the air that filled my nostrils. Shivering and shaking my head, I tried to remove the visions from my mind.

Tim nudged me from behind. "Zura, how are you? Are you alright? You are very quiet."

"I will be okay," I said. It's been a long day."

"Are you going to tell me what happened after Bain climbed down?"

"Bain must have thought that I fell the entire way, because he climbed back down as I said." I stalled.

"Then what happened?" Tim asked.

I knew Tim had questions, and he had a right to know, but I tried to keep out the details about the cracking of the bones and the skull.

"Tembo came, and I called out. He heard me and was upset by Bain's screaming. So, he killed him."

"Was it horrible?"

"It's not something I want to see or hear ever again."

"I am sorry you had to go through that, Zura."

"We will be home soon, and everything will be alright." I hoped.

I glanced behind us to see the entire herd following our procession. The uniformity of the color, combined with the elephants' size gave a feel of one body, moving as a single unit, with their ears flapping and tails flying. The low growling sounds they made as they stomped through the trees had little creatures scurrying for protection. They owned this place in the world. The true kings and queens of the jungle.

I knew it was only a matter of time before Tembo would be too old to stay in the herd, and would venture out to be all alone, or make a loose herd with other bull elephants. I couldn't bear the thought of Tembo being all alone or leaving the area. Maybe the reason he stayed with the herd so long was to be close to me. I reached out to touch his disfigured ear, running my hand over the peculiar curve of it. Tembo tried to reach behind with his trunk to touch me but could not reach.

Our house at Wild Hearts was in the distance. Tembo stopped when we exited the safety of the trees. When we cleared the trees, I saw my father's truck. He was home from his trip and probably frantic about Momma and me.

I became nervous to find out whether Momma had made it through her ordeal.

I was not afraid of monkeys, poisonous spiders or big cats. I feared nothing that maybe I should. The animals of the jungle were predictable. They followed the jungle rule. I knew I could out-climb them to escape being their next meal.

It turned out that I was afraid of the unknown. I didn't want to hear that Momma was no longer with us. I couldn't bear it if she died at the hands of Uncle. The beating of my heart, hard in my chest, the uneasiness of my stomach that was making flips, was making me hesitate. I wanted to slow down and not face what lay ahead of me. Whatever darkness loomed over me, I had to continue to move ahead—to travel through the present and deal with awaited at home.

I needed to keep Tembo moving.

"*Hoja*, Tembo. *Hoja!*" I demanded that he keep going.

Tembo obeyed my command and continued his slow pace.

Tim remained silent behind me. Maybe he too struggled with fear. His slender long arms snaked around me, and they shook.

I reminded myself that though I was used to the jungle and this life, Tim was not. He was probably petrified sitting on the back of such a gigantic creature.

"Are you alright, Tim?" I whispered.

"I'm trying to find some courage. I am afraid to fall off of Tembo and have the herd trample me like Bain. I am grateful not to have seen his body, and I'm sorry that you did." He hugged me from behind.

"We are going to be okay, Tim. We are almost home."

CHAPTER 10

Sitting on the porch with a glass in his hand was a familiar face. His scruffy beard and tattered clothes gave him away instantly. Lonnie smiled and laughed heartily.

"There she is! There's Jane!" Lonnie yelled as he rose and began to walk toward us as fast as his old bones would allow.

The workers all stopped their chores to eye the coming of the herd to deliver us home.

My father flew out of the screen door and stopped to watch the herd coming through the trees. Father stood there tall and sturdy with grief and fear etched all over his face. He seemed to break when he saw our procession. We must have been a glorious sight. Two children, sitting on the back of a magnificent beast, with a wild dog draped over the neck. And the herd following our lead.

Father ran toward us, visibly shaking. Tears rolled down his cheeks.

"Father!" I yelled and waved my good arm. "Father!"

"Zura! My girl! You are alright! You're alive!" he cried.

I searched for signs of her. Anything to tell me Momma was alive. I knew that if my mother were alive, nothing would stop her from getting to me. But I only saw my father, alone and crying. My pulse quickened and my whole body shook. Nothing could have prepared me for just seeing my father coming out of our house. My stomach burned, and my chest tightened when the sobs started. I was blinded by my tears and those moments of grief. I wiped my eyes on my dirty sleeve.

Tim hugged me tighter. "It is going to be alright, Zura. I've lost both of my parents. I know your pain. You are a survivor. You will survive this."

"She can't be dead," I sobbed. My grief came like a thunderous cloud, thick with rain, melting any little bit of sunshine I felt at seeing Tembo and then my father. Darkness filled my soul.

Father, not used to running a long distance, slowed his pace as his breath came heavy. He looked at me puzzled.

Just then, the screen door opened. With a cautious and hesitant gate, Momma stumbled out of the door. She wore her plain white nightgown that blew around her bare feet. She held on to the door for support as she righted herself. Her hair was loose and wild. It swirled and whipped as the wind carried it in an ocean wave of gold. Her one hand was on her shoulder; no doubt she was in pain from being shot. The other she held to her mouth in despair as she looked at me. She grabbed the porch railing for support and slowly made her way down the four steps. Her beautiful face showed anguish and a pang of sadness I had never seen before and hoped never to see again. She was overcome with her emotions and fell onto the muddy ground and began to crawl toward me, her sobs uncontrollable, her tears were like an uncontainable river rolling down her face. Nothing in the world was going to stop my mother from reaching me.

Father looked back and saw Momma crawling, and he ran back to her and lifted her into his arms. He placed a kiss on her head as she continued to sob. She cried for both of us. Neither knowing whether the other was still alive. Only speaking to each other in our dreams. Our connection temporarily broken in the physical form, but never in spirit. Our souls were connected for an eternity.

That day I learned that the bond between a mother and child is an unbreakable bond, no matter the distance; it held tighter than any rope imaginable.

As the elephants thunderously approached, with their large ears flapping and tails swaying back and forth, their lumbered gate would not be rushed for anyone.

Tembo obeyed my command when I told him to halt. The rest of the herd followed his lead, and we stood in the center of the field. I was cautious about taking the herd too close to the sanctuary or the house.

"Momma! Father! I called out to them as they approached. "Hello! Jambo!"

"Zura! Hello to you too. Oh, thank you God. Our child is home," my father called.

I waived my good arm over my head in greeting. Happy tears crawled down my dirty cheeks.

"Zura! My girl, we looked everywhere for you. Every day we searched. Lonnie told us what happened, and your mother has been frantic."

My heart leaped. "Momma."

Momma and I locked gazes, neither wanting to look away for fear the other would disappear. She smiled through her tears, and I smiled through mine.

My father laughed with his deep voice. "Yes, your Momma is going to be alright. You can see for yourself. I told her she could not get out of bed, but here she is, doing what she wants. To be honest," he whispered, "she is the worst patient I've ever had. At least my animal patients can't swear at me and throw a tantrum like your mother."

It made me giggle that Father was always the calm one and Momma was the one to react to things.

I was busting out of my skin to get to her. I had seen her get so many times in my head. I knew that having her hold me, I could put it to rest. At least that horrible memory could die.

"Okay, let me get down. Tembo, *chini.*" I said, and he bowed to my will. I still had Cha-cha in front of me. "You better get a muzzle," I warned, and the assistant disappeared into the infirmary. As soon as the muzzle was secured I said my goodbyes. "Cha-cha was stabbed, please take care of him," I instructed, kissing his muzzled face. I handed him to one of the assistants. "You be good, Cha-cha. Don't kill anyone, okay? These people will be helping you."

The anxious assistant shot me a nervous look, but Cha-cha was too tired and in pain to struggle.

Tim and I had help sliding off Tembo's back. Tim supported my weight, and we stood face to face with my parents. They eyed Tim cautiously, and he stood there looking numb, dirty, and exhausted.

Father put Momma down. Lonnie held on to her for stability. My father picked me up and swung me around. I just about fell into his arms. More from relief than injury. He felt wonderful and he hugged me tightly.

"Oh, thank goodness you are alright. We have been worried sick." Father looked past us and through the herd. "Where are the rest of the men? I have a few choice words for them if I am able to contain my rage."

Father looked at me, and I gave him a somber stare. "They are dead. Every last one of them. They won't be hurting anyone ever again."

"I see," Father cradled me in his arms. He quickly changed the subject, as if he knew how upset I was about the events in the jungle. "Momma said she has been dreaming of you and talking to you."

"I know, I heard her. I saw her too."

Father pulled me away from his shoulder to give me a peculiar look. "You saw her? How could you see her? She's been here the whole time."

"In my thoughts and my dreams. Momma was always there to comfort me. She told me to be fearless."

Momma rubbed my back. Still shaking and crying, she whispered. "Were you?"

"Was I what?"

"Fearless?"

"No, I was scared, pretty much all of the time, but I had my new brother to think about, right Tim?"

Tim held back. I am sure the moment was awkward and a little sad for him. He could never be reunited with his family in this lifetime. Maybe that was why I tried so hard to bring him into my family.

Father stood there staring at Tim like he was unsure what to make of him. The disheveled, tall, thin boy, with the messy hair, filthy from head to foot, looked like he would break down at any moment. Before my father could comment on Tim, I continued to stammer.

"I have to thank Tembo, Father. Before you stitch me up or tend to the wounds, or whatever else you need to do."

My father chuckled. "And, well, his whole family too, I guess. He brought them along for the ride. What a sight you made, coming out of the trees as you did. You looked like a fierce warrior." He patted Tembo's side.

Tembo growled and rubbed his trunk into my hair, and my father laughed even harder. "Alright, my Jungle Princess, say goodbye to Tembo so that we can get a look at these injuries. We have to clean them now before they get infected. There is another one of my patients that I know is probably busting out of her stitches right now," Father said, putting an arm around Momma.

I hugged Tembo's leg, and he let out a low growl.

"I missed you too. Thank you, my friend," I said, as he hugged me with his trunk. "You saved my life. When I needed you, you were my hero. I only hope that someday I can return the favor."

Tembo trumpeted in reply, and then he and his family turned and went back into the jungle. I knew then that I no longer had to stay away from him for him to become accepted into the herd. Tembo was safe for now in his family unit, and I couldn't wait to see him again.

My father carried me toward our home beside the sanctuary. Tim followed us wobbling from the stress on his ankle, and Lonnie helped my mother.

Father sat me on a kitchen chair, leaning down to analyze all of my injuries.

"How are you feeling?" he said. "My goodness Zura. You have cuts and scrapes everywhere. Your face is bruised like you smashed it into something."

"A tree and Bain's fist. Maybe more things, I lost count. Oh, I fell from Thinking Rock."

"You what?"

"It was when Bain almost shot me in the leg. He just brushed it though. That's when Cha-cha attacked him. The gun went off, and I got hit and fell."

"After you have had a chance to rest, we will sit down and talk about what has happened."

"I am dog tired. I hurt everywhere. Can I stay close to Momma?" I begged.

"Lonnie took Momma straight back to bed. She is resting, Zura. The bullet went into her left shoulder, and out the other side, so her muscles and shoulder joint need to heal. Not to mention that she has been weak and sick with worry over you."

"I have to see her. Even if it's for just a moment. Please, Father. Can we go there first?"

"Well, if you are sure that you can handle the pain for a few more minutes. But then we have to get these injuries tended to so they do not get infected."

"Okay, just a few minutes. The injuries have been there for a few days, and they hurt, but I just have to see her. Then I can rest."

"I understand completely. I don't think we've slept in days, from worriment over you. We searched everywhere. The men who were leading the group in the first place went looking for you where there was supposed to be a plane waiting for the hunting party to return. I searched the area near and around where your mother was shot in the field. I guess I went in the wrong direction. The authorities helped us as well. We had search parties from the nearby village looking, but no one could find you. Even Lonnie tried to direct us, but he couldn't remember any places beyond the field."

Father carried me into their bedroom. There she sat, propped up on pillows, her hair pulled back in a ponytail, her eyes exhausted. They perked up when she caught sight of me.

"Come here, let me get a look at you. Zura!"

"Momma!"

Father placed me on the edge of the bed next to Momma. Neither of my parents seemed to mind that I would be getting their sheets filthy. Even though I had a chance to wash some of the filth off, and the rains soaked me, the mud covered my body.

Momma's beautiful smile was all that I could focus on as she reached for me.

"Oh, my sweetheart, I have been so very worried about you." Momma hugged me close and I breathed in the familiar scent of her. "Zura, I have had dreams about you. I tried to focus on sending you positive thoughts."

"I know."

"You know? How do you know? You are filthy and all cut up. You look as though you have been through a war," she said as a tear rolled down her cheek. Not a sad tear, but a happy tear that I was finally home.

"I have been through a war, Momma. It was awful. But I heard you. I saw you in dreams. I heard your heart, I guess. I dreamed of you telling me to be strong. Momma! I missed you. I have been sick with worry about you. I saw them shoot you. I saw you fall. At first, when we arrived home, I thought you had died. But then I saw you come out of the house, and I knew we could heal together. Me and you. I've been so concerned."

Momma rearranged her blanket and motioned for me to sit on the side of the bed next to her.

"Oh, I have been afraid for you too. Your father and I have been a mess, trying to figure out how to get to you. We assumed that you would just find a tree and swing away."

"I couldn't," I said, looking over at Tim who stood in the doorway. "I couldn't leave him there."

"I see."

"Are you in a lot of pain, Momma?"

"I've had a very good doctor. Your father has been doting on me for days. He insists I am not strong enough to get out of this bed. But I feel almost completely healed, now that you are back. Well, maybe not completely healed," she said and placed her hand on her bandaged shoulder.

Momma pulled me to her. "I have been so scared for you. I am not sure what I would do if anything ever happened to you."

"I am alright, Momma. These wounds will heal."

"Not all wounds are on the outside."

"Yes, I know," I said hugging her tight. I whispered, hoping that only Momma would hear my confession. "I wanted them all to die. Is that bad, Momma? I feel ashamed."

"I know we always told you that it wasn't nice to wish ill on someone else. But in this case, Zura, you had to do what you had to do to survive. And if they were still alive, I would hunt them down and kill them all myself for hurting my little girl," Momma said, tightening her grip.

I believed that to be true. My mother was a warrior at heart. Her fierceness and protectiveness matched that of any big cat in the jungle, any mountain gorilla. Anything.

Father cleared his throat. "Alright, you two. The reunion is over; let's take a look at that leg, your shoulder, and your head. My child, is there a place on your body that isn't hurt?" Father took me from Momma's arms and carried me from the room.

"My heart is not hurt," I answered. "At least not now that I am home and Momma is alright."

My father didn't let go of me until he placed me on my bed. He re-examined me from head to toe.

"Nothing too serious, Zura. I'll ask one of the ladies to come in here and help you get cleaned up. We will take care of that nasty wound on your leg and that shoulder, okay?"

"Okay. But what about Tim? Will you look at him too? His ankle hurts him really bad."

"Yes, yes, of course I will. Now you get cleaned up and relax, okay? I will look at Tim here."

"Okay, I am so tired, that I don't think I can think straight. Can I see Momma again after you fix me up?"

"She has strict orders to stay in bed. Let's get you rested, and you can visit her later, okay?"

"Was she terribly worried?"

"Of course. We both were, Zura. But I knew that if ever a kid could make their way through the jungle, it would be you."

"How did you know what had happened to me?"

"Well, the three men from that hunting party came here after Momma was shot. They carried Momma to me, and explained that they knew of you, and knew that you were in the trees, but ignored you, because they were afraid of what the hunters would do to you if you were discovered.

"Because the men saved Momma's life, I agreed not to pursue their involvement in leading the men into the jungle to poach an elephant. They told us that when they turned to leave, you fell from the tree and they had to make a choice. The men knew that if you were okay, that you would be able to survive in the jungle, but Momma needed help immediately. They made a decision, and it saved her life. I will always be thankful."

"Please, can I see her again? Can I go and see Momma? I want to spend as much time with her until she can get out of bed."

"You need to rest first, remember? And I just have a few questions for you before we go to Momma again, starting with the young gentleman standing here."

Tim stood in the doorway, holding onto the door frame for support. He looked from me to Father. I could tell he was nervous.

"Don't you recognize him, Father? "He's my brother. He's your son." I lied easily.

Father stared at me. He glanced at Tim in confusion. "Zura, you are an only child. You don't have a brother."

"Not anymore. Father, did you ever meet someone and you just knew they were going to change your life?"

"Only twice in my life. The day I met my Rosie, and the day she gave me you," he said hugging me. "I guess I understand that the two of you have been through something very traumatic together, and that is sure to cause a connection, a bond. I understand."

"Father, he needs us. He is all alone in the world."

"I believe you said something like that the day you brought Cha-cha home," Father smiled.

"And look how wonderful that turned out. Cha-cha protected both of us. He is the most wonderful dog in the world."

"Well, I will be sure to thank him, from a distance, for protecting you, Zura."

"He would like that," I said.

It hurt pretty badly when he cleaned up my leg and reset my shoulder. Father said that I would be alright, I just needed to heal.

I tried to be tough, but I did cry from the pain.

Tim's ankle was wrapped up, and he was given something for the pain that made his eyes droopy. Instead of resting on a cot that Father set up in my room, Tim followed me around like a lost dog. I think he didn't want to be alone. His eyes were big and darting at the slightest sound like we were still being hunted.

Father picked me up and carried me into their bedroom. Tim followed closely behind but remained silent.

Momma was beaming when we entered the room. She sat up in bed, propped up with pillows, just like I had left her earlier. Her registers were lying on the bed next to her. She was studying her work but placed it on the pile of charts and journals when we entered the room.

Her hair was now pulled away from her face in a bun on the top of her head. Momma wore a fresh white cotton nightgown that made her look angelic. The muddy grime from crawling toward me in the muck was still on her forearm, but she was blind to it. Her mind was on her elephants, and probably me.

"Come here my sweet brave girl. Come here. I can see that it's you, now that you've removed some of that dirt; you still need a bath to get the rest of the filth off of you," she said and reached for me. I reached for her too, just like the day when my reach made me fall from the tree and into danger. It was with the same intensity and need for her. This time, she caught me as I fell into her arms. Momma rocked back and forth, cradling me like I was a baby again. In those moments, it was exactly what I needed. She pulled me away for a second and stared into my eyes. Trying to gauge my pain.

"Let me take another look at you. "You still look pretty beat up."

"You don't know the half of it," I said, as she brushed my unruly hair away from my eyes.

Tim awkwardly stood in the doorway of my parents' bedroom, still holding on to the wall for support. He looked sad, staring at the wood floor and not speaking. This caught Mom's attention.

"Who is this?" she questioned, eyeing Tim from across the room.

I looked at Tim and then back at my mother. "Why, Momma, maybe you don't recognize him under all that dirt. It's my brother. It's Tim! He is your son. Do you recognize him now?" I questioned, giving her a pleading gaze.

She looked intently at me, to a nervous Tim, and to my father's smiling face. We held our breaths and waited for her response. She smiled.

"Well, of course it is. Come here Tim, let me look at you closer."

Tim stood close to my mother's side of the bed and placed his hands in his pockets. Mother looked intently at Tim for several seconds before she answered.

"Yes, I see you now. It must have been the lighting," she lied. "Hmm, you have the same brown hair. Just like Zura's hair," she said, scuffing up his disheveled hair as she continued. "It must have been the trauma of being shot. Please, remind me again how old you are. I am sorry, Tim, I must have forgotten," she said with a wink to me.

Tim blushed at the attention. "I'm almost a man, now. I'm twelve. Turned twelve a few months ago," he said.

"Of course, you are," Momma smiled, and hugged Tim. "Welcome home, son."

Father interrupted our reunion.

"Why don't you two get cleaned up, let your mother rest, and we will talk about your adventures after dinner when you both have had time to rest."

After our baths, we sat on my bed. I was in my stretchy shorts and one of Father's old shirts. Tim borrowed a much-too-big, pair of Father's shorts and shirt. Father belted the shorts for Tim with rope.

"How are you feeling, Little Sister?" Tim asked.

"I am alright, you?"

"You know, you didn't have to do that."

"Do what?"

"Make your mother lie about me being her son. I am no sooner her son than Tembo."

"You most certainly are. You are now a part of this family, Tim. You saw Father's face. He was proud to have a son. And so is Momma. You have a place here, Tim. It is your home, now."

He shook his head in silence and laid next to me, just like in the jungle, and we took a nap side by side. No ropes to bind us. We didn't need them anymore.

It was almost dark when we woke to the amazing smell of food. My stomach growled as I nudged Tim to wake. "You smell that? She's making one of my favorite meals. Let's eat!"

We both ran into the kitchen looking for the aromatic dish. Mother, with the help from Lonnie, made us a dinner of porridge, chicken *muamba*, and root vegetables. They were all my favorites.

"Momma, it smells amazing, but should you be out of bed?" I questioned as I lifted the pot to breathe in the aroma of spices in the dishes.

"Oh, I am fine. Lonnie helped with the things that I needed two arms to do. Your father, you know how he worries. Honestly now that you…"

"And Tim," I added quickly.

"…are home, I feel much better. My heart has healed. It was broken thinking that I might have lost you."

Tim and I set the plates on the table. Momma put the food into big bowls and we all sat down to eat.

Father was curious to hear our stories. We excitedly shared the information in unison, each adding a portion like a tag team; both of us stumbling over each other's words and laughing. It was good to laugh again.

Lonnie was actually the first to start the story.

"Warren is my friend, was my friend, and an avid hunter. He had more money than he knew what to do with, so we went hunting. Warren would use that money to bribe the right people to get what he wanted. In this case, Warren wanted an elephant's head to place on his kill wall. One with big tusks. But when your mother stood in front of his prize, he never stopped firing that rifle and that caused the chain of events that led to all their deaths. I suppose that if I had not made my way through the field, I would also have been dead. Right, Jane?"

I bowed my head in shame and only nodded.

"It's alright, child, I have to live with the guilt that I didn't do something to free you. I am so sorry, Jane," he said, and I raised my head and nodded again.

"I am glad Uncle is dead," Tim interrupted dispassionately.

Lonnie placed a comforting hand on Tim's shoulder.

"Yes, well, I saw a whole other side of Warren on this trip, but we should never wish another person dead. It was the first time Warren brought his man, Bain, on a trip with us, and it was to rid himself of this brave boy right here."

"Bain was supposed to kill me," Tim clarified and shoveled more food into his mouth.

Lonnie shook his head. "I will never understand why he thought it appropriate to hurt anyone. That evil side of him came out in that jungle, and I made up my mind that I could not be a part of it. When I learned that Jane, uh, err, Zura, understood every word that was said, and that she led us right back to where it all started, I saw the opportunity to try to get help. I knew that if I tried to take the children with me, that Bain would just shoot me and maybe the children. After they realized that Zura was not going to lead them out, I would be of no use to anyone. But, if I could get to a safe area and find others to help me, I could free them both from the clutches of Warren and Bain."

Mother looked at Lonnie inquisitively. "Jane? Why Jane?"

It was my turn to add to the story.

"I'm Jane. They called me Jane because they didn't know my name. I did not speak to the men and hid the fact that I understood them so that they would relax around me. So that I could learn about their plans for me."

"Clever, Zura," my father said. "Very brave girl."

"She was amazing!" Tim joined in. "She climbed trees and was able to spot danger everywhere we went. Zura made me the most amazing hot tea from leaves that she found in the jungle. Zura also made sure I ate, hid Cha-cha and me behind the waterfall, and didn't even cry out when Bain put her shoulder back into place. She didn't cry when she fell from the tree. She was just simply amazing."

"So were you," I said giving him a bashful smile.

My father looked confused. "*Behind* the falls? What do you mean, *behind* the falls? I never saw anything else in that area."

I nodded my head. "Yes, there is a cave behind it. No one else knows it is there. I've been in there lots of times before. It seemed like a perfect place to put Tim and Cha-cha, while I dealt--"

I stopped my explanation when I saw my mother's face grow pale. "To do what exactly?"

"Anything I had to do," I answered bravely.

"When you say *anything*, what do you mean?"

"Momma, I tried to escape without hurting anyone. But after I knew that they would kill both Tim and me. I had to follow the law of the jungle. Kill or be killed. Eat or be eaten."

"And did you?" Momma asked cautiously.

"Kill?"

Momma nodded.

"Not directly, no."

"We tried," Tim added, and I rolled my eyes at him.

Father leaned on his elbows. "Are you saying that the two of you tried to kill someone?"

I swallowed hard from my shame. "Well, just one. Bain. He wanted to murder Tim for the money and me for the fun of it. I couldn't let it happen. He also shot Otis in the back for no reason at all. He was an evil man. I can't believe that he actually has a son and he would try to hurt us."

Lonnie put down his fork. "Otis is dead too?"

"They are all dead," I said. "Every last stinking one of them."

Momma took a drink of water and slowly placed her cup on the table.

"Can you explain what you mean by your statement about trying to kill Bain?"

"Sure," I said dispassionately. "Bain caught up to us after Tim hurt his ankle and we couldn't run away. I had gotten careless. When I told Bain that Uncle was going to die from the water he was drinking and that he was going to lose all the promised money, he became nervous and angrier than his usual state. So, he wanted us to go and find Uncle. We located his dead body, and from the bite marks, I suspected Cha-Cha had killed him.

"I always told you that dog was a wild animal and not a pet dog," Father interrupted.

"No. You are wrong. Father," I continued. "Cha-cha killed Uncle, to protect us. He saved us from one more man trying to kill us. I will always be grateful to Cha-cha for saving us from Uncle and Bain.

"When Cha-cha caught up with us, he was covered in blood. We cleaned him off in the stream, and the only wound I found was the knife injury from Bain. Most of the blood was around his muzzle. Since Bain was still alive and chasing us, it had to be Uncle's."

"I see," Momma answered, growing even paler.

"That only left Bain for us to deal with. When he threatened to shoot one of us if the other got out of line, we both knew that we had to do something drastic if we were going to make it. When we camped, Bain fell asleep. I took the knife from my pocket, cut the rope that bound the two of us, circled the camp and hesitated too long before attempting to stab Bain in the heart. He grabbed the knife and I only managed to stab him in the shoulder. I fell backward with the knife and hit him over the head with a rock before he could get up. That's when we found Cha-cha and cleaned him up at the water; that's when I pieced together that Cha-cha killed Uncle."

Father placed his elbow on the table and held his chin. Worriment showed on his face. "Where did you get a knife? You were bound together?"

"Yep, the whole time. The men tied me around the waist. The other end was tied to Tim's wrist. After Bain stabbed Cha-cha with the knife, it fell to the ground. I guess when Cha-cha ran off, it must have released because of all of his thick fur."

"But how did you end up with it?" Father questioned.

"I pretended to trip, picked it up and put it in my pocket. Bain never suspected that I was anything more than a clumsy kid."

Tim broke his silence. "She was amazing! Sometimes I wondered whether she was also part wild animal, like Cha-cha."

Momma laughed. "Sometimes, I wonder the same thing. What did you do next, Zura?"

"We got to the stream below the falls and cleaned off Cha-cha. I knew I could hide the both of them in the cave, so we climbed up and into the cave. While Bain was out cold from the rock I'd hit him with, we stole his backpack and I found a flashlight in it for Tim to use. Tim feared the bats, but I think he was very brave to stay with Cha-cha and take care of him. Cha-cha loves Tim too," I smiled at Tim.

"In my mind, I knew that I could out-climb Bain at Thinking Rock and that maybe he would fall off the cliff, or I could push him or something. I never expected that even if he had a chance to shoot me that he would be able to do it with us at the top.

"Even though Cha-cha was hurt and in pain, he came to find me and left poor Tim alone in the cave with the bats. Cha-cha circled like he always did when we would race to see which one of us could get to the top first. He attacked Bain again and the gun went off. As you know, the bullet grazed my leg. All I knew was that even though I was scared and tired and hungry, I had to get rid of Bain before he killed us. And he was mad, mad as a killer bee. Crazy too. He was screaming and looking for me. After I fell, he climbed back down, thinking I was at the bottom, but I landed on a small ledge and remained still until I heard the elephant herd moving through the trees.

"When I saw Tembo, I yelled for him. He was upset by Bain's yelling. I like to think that he knew I was in danger, and that's why he killed Bain. Tembo speared him and stomped him into the ground. I probably should have been sad that someone else died. But I was relieved. It meant that I could stop running from them and get home. And you know the rest."

My parents were speechless for several minutes. They searched for the words to either help me feel better about everything or help themselves deal with what they just learned. In the end, they were silent. And that was alright with me. Sometimes there are just no words.

CHAPTER 11

It was so good to be back at Wild Hearts.

Days turned into weeks as everyone settled back into a routine.

Things were different. We had two more people that quickly engaged in our daily activities.

My parents were more protective, always looking at me with sideways glances of concern. They changed their focus to always wanting to know where I was and what I was doing. I understood why. They were afraid to lose me. My freedom to roam the jungle had ended with the dead men.

My leg barely even bothered me, but the wound left a scar. My shoulder was healed, and the cut on my head only showed a thin white line next to my hairline. I was strong again. At least physically.

Mentally, though, my struggles were still in my nightmares, and sometimes they crept into my daydreams. At night, in my dreams, I am swinging in the trees, fast and powerful and happy. I am racing the monkeys, high in the trees. But in a moment of panic, the trees in front of me disappear, and I begin to fall. Sometimes into a pit of snakes, other times, lions are waiting to devour me. The worst is when Bain is waiting to shoot me. He is screaming my name over and over, telling me he is going to kill me.

Momma says that it's just my brain processing the horror that I survived. That would be true if I didn't jump from sudden sounds, or when I am alone. I was always looking over my shoulder for Bain or Uncle to grab me and put me back into that time.

Those experiences changed me in several other ways too. I did not visit Thinking Rock or the waterfall. They were no longer places of peace for me. They are now filled with death and terror. I was afraid that even after the time that had passed, that Bain would still be there. Of course, I knew that would never be possible because Tembo had crushed his body. But the fear was alive and controlling my actions. I was still a prisoner on some level and forever changed.

I chose to stay close to home, maybe out of fear of what memories would come alive even though I tried very hard to erase them.

Evenings were always a bonding time for my family. I would sit with my mother and tell her about my dreams of being a princess, and we would make up stories together about all of the wondrous things we would do together. I could picture us dancing and twirling in our long gowns and laughing as we spun.

Having Tim and Lonnie with us added to the excitement. They told stories about the United States. Wonderful stories about a city called Chicago, about California and New York City. They each told stories of their homes. I became fascinated with thoughts of fashion—with something called a flapper. I was excited to learn that women also preferred their hair short in something called a bobbed hairstyle. They wore jewels and red lip stain. The people loved to dance too. Favorite dances were called the Shimmy and the Toddle. Lonnie was friends with an actor named Charlie Chaplin who appeared in movies where nobody talked.

We learned that Uncle was part of something called a mob. As an attorney, Lonnie's job was to find ways to keep Uncle out of trouble. It explained why Uncle had a man like Bain, who was a killer, on his payroll.

Lonnie and Tim settled into the routine. The daily chores were easier with more hands to help. Lonnie helped with the feedings of the elephants, the clean-up, and shoveling of dung. He said it was penancing to clean their dung after being a part of the hunting of such beautiful creatures. I agreed.

Lonnie and I had a good relationship and spent a lot of time caring for the elephants together. He told me stories of his life when he was a young father. A tear came to his eye when he shared how much he missed his wife who died a few years earlier, and his son, who never spoke to him because they'd had a falling out over Lonnie's friendship with Uncle.

"Why don't you go and visit him?" I asked.

"Because he doesn't want to see me. I wasn't always the kind of father that he needed me to be. Always traveling, drinking too much, and never there for him. Now that I am older and retired, I have the time, but he resents the many years I wasn't there for him. Can't say as I blame him."

"Maybe someday, you can try again. Keep trying until he gives in and agrees to see you. Then you could apologize to him."

"You really are a clever girl, Zura. Figured that out the minute I found that bullet and the tree limb. I still don't know how you managed to keep your wits about you."

"Oh, I was scared of the men. Especially Bain. He terrified me. But I am no quitter. You can't get something done by only thinking about it. You gotta go out and do it. That's why I am such a good climber. I had a lot of practice. Every day, I would sneak off when my father was gone, and my mother focused on the herd."

"Weren't you scared?"

"Sometimes. Like when I got careless, and there would be a lion close by, or a gorilla. Gorillas and lions terrify me. But I don't let my fear stop me from doing what I want to do. I just go out and do it. It's simple."

"Zura, you are the bravest girl I have ever met, and smart way beyond your years. I wish we would have met under better circumstances."

I thought about that statement for a moment. "How would we have ever met?"

Lonnie thought long and hard as well. "Good point. I guess we wouldn't." He laughed and ruffled my hair. "You don't climb anymore, do you?"

I met his question with silence. The words wouldn't come.

Tim poured over books with Father. He spent a great deal of time learning about the business, about being a veterinarian, and how the sanctuary worked on donations. Tim reviewed Father's textbooks from his time at Michigan State University. He left the care of the elephants to Lonnie and me so that he could bond with my father. I suspected he was missing his parents.

About a week after my father and Lonnie returned from a trip to rescue some orphaned babies, I heard my father tell my mother that old Lonnie broke down and cried when he saw the recent carnage of a mother elephant and orphaned babies. He went from the hunter to the savior. Lonnie said that he would devote the rest of his life to saving the elephants.

Everything was perfect, full of happiness with Lonnie and Tim as part of our family.

Tim was intense with his teachings, and he always had his nose in a book, just like Momma.

On a pleasant day in December, I was sitting in a stall in one of the holding pens, enjoying some quiet time with Cha-cha, when I heard Lonnie come into the barn. He was talking to one of the new baby elephants that were recently rescued. He fed the baby with a large bottle and rubbed the top of one of the elephant's heads.

"You better slow down your swallowing, Little One. You don't want to upset your belly." The baby elephant continued to drink hastily. "You must miss her, don't you? Your mother. You know I used to be one of those men. I didn't care what I shot. I called it a sport. I did it for the pelts, for the tusks, for the fun of it. Never with a conscience of what my actions did to the ones left behind. Little ones like you. I can't fix what I've done in the past. But I can make sure that you get the chance to grow up. There you go, you drank the whole thing," Lonnie said, removing the bottle from the elephant's mouth.

He placed the bottle on the floor and rubbed the elephant, giving her much needed contact and attention.

"I promise to send the money. You will be taken care of, my new friend. Until my dying breath, I will devote my money, my life, and the rest of my time here on this earth taking care of this place so that you always have a home.

"He will help with the money he inherited. We worked it out, and it is going to be fine, once the girl adjusts. She will understand that it is for the best. But it's going to be hard for her for a while, so be her friend, and love her like her brother does." He took the bottle and turned to leave. When he did, he caught sight of me and looked surprised.

"Oh, Jane, I didn't see you there."

"It's Zura! Don't ever call me that again!" My words exploded.

"I am sorry. That was very insensitive of me. You just startled me."

I didn't care about his apology.

"Tell me what you meant by devoting your money to this place. What is going on? Are you going somewhere? You can't go. You just got here. And you still have to teach me how to beat you in chess. I'm getting better, but I still can't beat you. Lonnie, please don't go!"

"Zura, we have a lot of work to do. Seeing what it takes to keep this place running, seeing how much the funds are needed and how hard your parents try every year to find the money to take care of these animals, we have the means to make sure the animals you save will always have a home. I'm too old to make amends for all of my sins, but some may be forgiven if I can devote the rest of my life to saving these creatures. Think of Betty. She needs my help."

"Betty? Who is Betty?"

"Oh, it's the new baby your father brought in the other day. She changed my life. This place changed my life—*you* changed my life. You fought harder to stay alive in that jungle than I have fought for anything in my entire life."

I stopped petting Cha-cha and stood. I brushed the straw from my clothes and walked over to where Lonnie stood. "What does that mean?"

"It means that we are leaving. We are going to make a better life for you, for this place, and all of the animals you save. That's my promise."

My heart raced. I didn't want to know the answer to the question I was about to ask. "We?"

Lonnie stalled. "Zura, why don't we go up to the house and find your parents and talk about this together."

"No! Answer my question. Who is we?" But I knew the answer. I ran into the house screaming his name. "Tim! Where are you? Tim!" I searched every room in the empty house. Then it dawned on me where he spent most of his time, and I made my way to my father's office. I opened the door with a bang, out of breath and distraught.

"Zura," my father jumped at the banging of the door against the wall. "Take it easy, Zura. You scared us half to death."

He stopped to examine my face and looked just as worried. "What's happened? What's wrong?"

I stood there unsure whether I was angry at Tim for wanting to leave, or despair at the thought of losing my brother. At that moment, I picked angry. It was a much easier emotion to deal with than despair.

"You!" I pointed at a stunned Tim. "You lied to me! You said you were my brother. Siblings don't go off and leave their families. Tell me it's not true." I was pushing down the despair. "Tell me!" I balled my fists at my side.

"Zura," he managed to say. He dropped his head and looked at the floor.

Father tried to control the situation. "Let's all calm down and talk about this rationally," he said in a soft calm voice.

"No!" I screamed through my tears and ran from the room. I ran to the field, the one where I almost lost my mother. I ran through the jungle. The jungle where I saw all of the people die. I ran to the waterfall where I hid Tim and Cha-cha.

With Thinking Rock in front of me, I scaled it quickly, just like the day I ran for my life. I was running again. Escaping the fear of losing Tim. This time, no one was chasing me to kill me, but it didn't mean that it was less painful.

When I cried it out, I looked from my favorite spot. I glanced into the world in front of me. The top of Thinking Rock. I had gone there for years when I needed to sort things out. But I soon realized that being there brought back bad memories of Bain and Uncle.

Thoughts like watching Bain shoot Otis and of Jasper's labored death were running rapidly through my brain. Thinking Rock looked different to me now. It too had changed. Thinking Rock was no longer part of my enjoyment, of my quest for conquering. It was a horrific memory that still haunted my days and crept into my nightmares. I knew I could never find peace from its cliffs again. It would never hold the same meaning for me. I had to let it go.

I looked down from the top and remembered the pain of the bullet grazing my leg. Thinking I was going to die, over and over again, in those few days, did something to me. But I didn't die, I survived. Maybe out of sheer stubbornness, maybe it was knowing that Tim couldn't possibly make it without me. He had become important in such a short period of time. If I were honest with myself, I would say that I saw the sadness in his eyes. I saw the way that he looked at me like he wanted permission. I put my selfish needs ahead of his.

Looking down from my height, I could see Tim approaching, and he stopped for a moment at the waterfall. He looked up and let out a visible shiver. The place scared him. The fact that Tim followed me into the jungle was saying how much he cared about me. I remembered that he was a faster runner than me, so I knew he had tracked me.

I climbed down to face him, or maybe to try to change his mind.

His eyes were gloomy, but his appearance was clean and neat, except for the too-big shorts he insisted on wearing.

"Zura, you know that I don't belong here." He raised his hands to the heavens. "This is *your* world, Jungle Girl, not mine. My uncle had only one living relative—me. Now I have a lot of money, more money than I would need for many lifetimes. And there is nothing I want more than to help keep this place running forever. I cannot do that from here. I also want to follow in Father's footsteps. I want to be a veterinarian. My home is in the United States, not here. That's where I can get the education that I need to make a difference. Let me go so that I can do my part to save the animals. Let me do this, please."

"You can't go, Tim. We are your family now. You're my brother."

"No, Zura, I am not. I'm just a boy that you happened to be bound to for a few days."

His words stung. "You are so much more than that to me. And you *are* my brother!"

"Zura, I have no family. I am alone. Well, I was until Lonnie volunteered to help me sort this all out at home. He is an attorney, you know. He was Uncle's attorney for years. He helped keep Uncle out of trouble many times. You can go back to the way it was before. Way before you met me. You can afford to lose me, Zura."

His words stung. They hurt worse than any fall from a tree, from any bullet piercing my leg. I felt broken and wished for that rope that bound us together. I watched, as it all became unraveled and my heart broke with his words.

"Don't say that! I can't lose you. We are alive because of each other. We kept each other going."

"Try to understand."

"I will never forgive you if you leave, Tim," I said and started walking home. Tim followed closely behind me.

"That's unfair, Zura. And selfish. Can't you tell how much I am suffering being here? How is it that you have such a keen sense of everything when you are in the jungle? You see the danger. You hear all of its sounds. But, you can't see my misery, my hurt. I am not doing this for just myself. I am also doing this for you. I will be making sure that the money flows to the sanctuary for anything that is needed and more."

I stopped and turned to look at him.

"But, you could have an amazing life here, with me, with Momma, and Father. We love you, and we can make you happy."

"No, I need to make *myself* happy. I need to deal with this. I am looking over my shoulder every few minutes. I am scared all of the time."

I knew he was right. I saw that look of fear many times in his eyes.

"Tim, what about Cha-cha? If you leave him now, it will break his heart."

"Nice try. Cha-cha may like me, but he will always be your dog. I am sure he will be just fine in your care."

I was out of fight. I knew Tim was right. How could I be so selfish when I knew he had to heal himself? I couldn't put my need to keep him close above his need to get as far away from the jungle as he could. The entire thing mixed my emotions into a brewing storm.

We walked back to the house in silence. Neither knowing what to say to each other to make things better.

When we reached the house, I went into my room and slammed the door. I felt like being a dramatic kid who couldn't deal with one more bad thing happening.

My mother left me alone for an hour or so, but then she knocked on my door and tried to make me understand.

"Can I come in?" She asked.

"I just want to be alone."

"Zura, you have to understand," she spoke through the door. "Tim is not happy here. You grew up here. This world is a part of you. Tim was forced to come, and he witnessed things that he should never have to see."

"I saw the same things," I answered in defiance.

"Yes, you did, sweetheart. Now let me come in and we will sort this out."

Momma took my silence as an invitation to enter my room. She sat on my bed next to me and stroked my hair.

"Come here, Sweetheart," Momma said, and I reached for her. She hugged me close and kissed my head. "I understand how upset you are; we are as well. But think of Tim. He lost his parents, and then the only other living relative didn't want him. Can you understand how that might make him feel?"

"But we want him. He can have a family here."

Momma grabbed my hands and moved me away from her embrace so she could look into my eyes.

"Tim will always remember you, Zura. He is doing this for you. Tim wants to take care of you and your home in the only way he thinks he can be helpful."

"I'll never see him again. It's tearing out my heart to know he will go and never come back."

"Zura, you don't know that. When he is ready, he will come back."

"No, he will not."

"Let's just take one step at a time, alright?"

Tim knocked but didn't wait to be invited into the room. He had his hands in his pockets, but gone was the boy that stared at the floor. He seemed confident in his decision, and relieved.

"I'll write to you all of the time. I will tell you all about the United States, and you can tell me what is going on here. We can still communicate through letters. After I figure this out, I want to get my education. I will be back. I promise."

"Don't make promises that you won't keep."

"Zura, I promise, okay?"

I nodded at him, knowing he was right.

Part of growing up was knowing that not everything revolved around you. Sometimes others had to come first, even if you don't like it.

The day Tim left was one of the hardest days of my life. He just kept telling me it was for the best.

He hugged me goodbye and whispered, "Goodbye, Little Sister. I'll never forget you." With that, he turned away from me and left the jungle behind. He left the pain and terror of our time together. I was standing there with a gigantic piece of my heart missing.

It took me several weeks to get past that day. The worst scar was the emptiness I felt that Tim chose to leave. But he was gone. And so, I was forced to move on.

Weeks after he left, I received a letter from Tim.

He wrote:

Zura,

I hope this letter finds you well and mended. I think about you every day and know that I made the right decision in leaving. Lonnie is helping me to sort out the financial things, and we hired a tutor to teach me at the house. It's more room than Lonnie and I need so I am selling it. I just want a small home in the country somewhere, Quiet and maybe a place with trees and lots of flowers. It will remind me of you.

You will be happy to know that I gutted the trophy room. I couldn't stand to see all those hunted animals staring at me. And I felt that I would be dishonoring my time with you if I kept them on the wall. I donated them to a museum so that I didn't have to ever look at them again.

How is Momma feeling? How are you feeling? Tell Father I miss our talks.

Please answer me, Sister. I miss you. Hug Cha-cha for me.
Give Momma and Father my best.
Love,
Tim

I wrote back to Tim immediately, telling him all about Tembo's herd and how much time I was spending with him. Cha-cha's hunting adventure when he brought a zebra's leg onto our porch and started to eat it, causing Momma to scream at him through the screen door. I told him about the new truck my Father was able to get with donations and how much I missed him.

We wrote every month for about a year. Tim would tell me about Lonnie and him and their travels and his schooling. I would write to him about the herd, including the new ones, like Tembo's older brother Kendi, who looked just like his brother, except for the difference in their right ear. Kendi was too old to become part of the female family. Tembo was starting to join the males more, leaving the predominately female herd to raise the babies. He was growing up and moving on.

As time went on, the letters became fewer and fewer. What started as a monthly excitement to get news from Tim, stretched on for months and then one day they just stopped coming. I was sure that Tim had moved on with his life and left me in the painful past.

CHAPTER 12

August 1930

My experiences gave me a renewed passion for the plight of the elephants and I became as obsessed with saving them as my Mother and Father. Wild Hearts Elephant Sanctuary became my fixation.

I worked with Momma for years, learning all that she could teach me. Filling up my journals of observations, charts and medical information for the elephants that stayed at our sanctuary, and Tembo's herd. He chose to be alone most of the time, wandering the jungle and showing up when he wanted to.

I outgrew the need to climb the trees and race the monkeys. At twenty-one, I left all my childhood foolishness behind me. Well, except for riding on Tembo. That was an enjoyment I could not refuse. His favorite thing to do was to go to the river with me on his back and spray me with water. I laughed every time he did it.

Momma would walk behind us and capture it in pictures.

I went on with my life and made tremendous strides, but I no longer wished to see the waterfall and its painful memories.

Tembo's old family grew in numbers and size. I watched the elephant herd grow. At least in our area of Africa. Other places still did not protect the elephants, and poachers butchered the gentle giants.

Mother and I could sit together with our books for hours in mutual silence. We always made sure that we were not separated again. It was too painful for either one of us to think about the time when we both wondered whether the other was dead or alive.

Father still traveled and brought elephants home that needed his help. He never stopped his quest, and that devotion that both of my parents followed was a role model for me all of my life.

And then there was my beloved dog. Cha-cha, slowed down in his later years. Mostly he hung out on the porch. Occasionally he would chase some chickens. But his time in the jungle was over.

One day, I was sitting on our porch with Cha-cha, petting him. He looked up at me with his aging eyes that had filmed over into almost blindness. No longer fierce, he was as tame as any family pet. Even Father could be seen petting Cha-cha from time to time. Father didn't like anyone to know that he had a soft spot for Cha-cha after he'd saved my life.

That day, Cha-cha climbed up onto my lap and licked my hand. I rubbed his neck and his back and kissed his head.

"What's the matter, boy?" I said to him.

His body went slack and I felt his last breath leave his body. Just as quickly as he came into my life, he vanished. My fierce protector, my loyal wild dog was lifeless in my arms. I buried my head in his fur and cried the loss of him. Never would there be a more protective friend than my sour dog named Cha-cha. Oh, how I loved him and missed him.

We buried him on the hill behind the house, where nothing could disturb his eternal slumber. I made a cross and a plaque that read, *Cha-cha, my love, my protector, my friend.*

My Father, who had originally been completely against keeping Cha-cha, cried at his funeral. As always, my Father was my rock, my shoulder to cry on, and the person who would always listen to my heartbreak.

In the months that followed Cha-cha's death, I couldn't help but think back to the time that he saved me from the evil man, Bain. And then thoughts of Tim would creep into my mind. I couldn't help but wonder where he lived and what he looked like after ten years. As soon as I thought of him, I pushed him right out of my mind. He decided to lose contact with me and move on. He never returned.

Mother always said someday he would find his way back. I didn't believe it. Ten years was a long time and memories faded to dust.

One evening when Father was not traveling, we sat around the table after dinner. Father placed his spectacles on his face and grabbed a letter from his shirt pocket.

"I received this today," he said, opening the letter. "It says that our dear friend, Lonnie, has died. He went peacefully in his sleep."

Father placed his hand on mine to comfort me. As much as I liked Lonnie, he was a reminder of things I would carry with me for my whole life.

"Who sent the letter?" I asked, wiping a tear from my eye.

Father ignored my question and folded the letter.

"Let's have a toast to Lonnie. Our friend, we will miss you. You saved many of our elephants with your generosity. We will always miss you. To Lonnie." Father raised his glass, and we followed suit.

Lonnie was a special person to us all. Though it saddened me, I was so grateful to have known him. After all those years, I kept the bullet casing that he had handed to me on that day in the jungle. I remembered thinking he was crazy to walk out into the field with the wildebeest. Lonnie had the richest laugh. It made me smile to think about him. He was a kind and a gentle man.

He went home to make sure that the sanctuary would survive, and now it is thriving. The funds were always there for anything we needed, but not for expanding our need to tell the world about the atrocities facing the lives of our beloved beasts.

Lonnie did what he had set out to do. The penance was fulfilled. Old Lonnie could rest in eternal peace.

CHAPTER 13

August 23rd is my birthday. It's the day when my parents reflect on my birth, their meeting, and when they tell embarrassing stories of my childhood. Little stories. Stories that are nothing more than uncomfortable for me but great memories for them. We never discuss *the big story,* even though it shows in my mother's eyes from time to time. I would catch her looking at me in a way that could only be described as mother's guilt. In those moments, Momma looked as though she blamed herself for what happened to me so long ago. In truth, sometimes I accused her as well. If she would have been more attentive, I may not have been in the jungle. It was unfair to blame her for my curiosity. But sometimes I did.

I never worked up the courage to have that conversation with her. Maybe someday I would find the strength to tell Momma and work through those awful feelings. I needed closure.

Now that so much time has passed, we act as though that time was just a bad dream. Almost like it never happened. To be honest, I sometimes think that is true. Some bad dream that haunts my nights.

I woke to an incredible smell of cinnamon and coffee. Forgetting to make my bed, I threw on some shorts and a tee shirt, pulled my long hair back in a ponytail, and raced to the kitchen.

Momma woke extra early to make breakfast. She usually started her days before the sun came up ever since Father bought her a new stove. He teased that she loved that stove more than she loved him.

The stove was the most modern item in our home. It could burn wood or coal, and had four top burners with a lid that could be folded down to give Momma another work surface. The stove had an oven and a broiler. Its exterior was beautiful, with its cream color and marbled green accents.

Momma made eggs and her porridge called *putupap*. She added her own flare to the African dish, with cinnamon, clove, and nutmeg. It made the house smell incredible. She made mealie bread, which is a cornbread, and served it with fresh honey.

"Good morning, birthday girl," she said, planting a kiss on my cheek.

"Morning Momma," I smiled. "This house smells amazing!"

"Well, you can thank your Father for giving me this wonderful gift that has inspired me to get creative with my cooking. Have a seat. Your breakfast is ready."

"Where is Father?"

"Oh, Peter left before the sun came up. He said he had to go and pick up your birthday present."

"I hope it's a new truck."

"Zura, you know that your father isn't going to buy you a vehicle." Momma spooned out her porridge into a bowl and placed it in front of me. She gave herself a small bowl of it and sat across from me.

I ate two big spoonsful of the porridge.

"I want to get an early start on charting the new baby brought in yesterday. Do you know who he reminds me of?"

"I saw it too. The baby looks like Tembo, like Kendi does. A younger brother maybe?" Momma answered.

"Well, that would be great to have a lot of little Tembo's running around here. Kendi is much older than Tembo, but a beautiful copy of his little brother. I think the baby is Kendi's. He is smaller than some of the other babies, but someday he will be just as magnificent as Tembo and Kendi. I still can't get Kendi to let me ride him as Tembo does. Maybe because he never grew up in a sanctuary." I broke off a piece of the cornbread and poured extra honey on to it and shoved it in my mouth, enjoying the warm rich bread and the sweetness of the honey on my tongue.

"Momma, you killed the bread. It is so delicious that I want to eat the whole thing."

"Why thank you, Zura. I am also working on an extra special birthday dinner for you."

"Don't trouble yourself, Momma. I appreciate it, but you don't have to go all out for my birthday. It's not like it's a special one."

"Yes, I do. This one will be special, every one of your birthdays is special to me," Momma said with a smile. Momma was unusually giddy.

Father's truck could be heard coming down the dirt road. I broke off another massive piece of bread and started to pour honey on it when I heard heavy steps walking on the porch.

"Bet Father will want some of this amazing bread. I better have another piece before he…"

The words caught in my throat when the door opened and Father walked in slapping the back of a much taller and even more handsome Tim.

I stared awkwardly at him, unable to speak.

"Do you like a little honey with your bread, Little Sister?" He said with a deep, rich, and confident voice.

His words brought me back to reality. I looked down and realized I was still pouring the honey onto my bread, and it filled my plate.

My tears came quickly, blinding my eyes. My emotions were a combination of anger and joy. Anger for the years of forgetting about me. Joy for standing in the kitchen, home with me again.

I was unable to speak, unable to move when I sucked in my breath and held it. When I closed my eyes and opened them again, it was the same. Tim, all grown up.

He no longer had that messy brown hair. He kept it neatly trimmed and combed. His eyes were the same brownish color, but wiser. They no longer held that wide, scared look. Now they were relaxed and confident.

Tim stood as tall as my father, with broad shoulders and a wickedly handsome smile.

His suit looked expensive, long gone were the borrowed shorts held up by a rope. He was the same, but completely different. Then again, so was I.

I dreamt for years of seeing him again, and there he stood, back in my life.

We stared at each other for what seemed like an eternity. Both assessing each other.

He smiled and moved forward, and I ran to him and wrapped myself around him. I didn't care that there were two strangers standing beside Tim. My focus was on him. Everyone else vanished, and he became my entire focus.

I released him, but he pulled me toward him and placed his arm over my shoulder. "Let me get a look at you, Little Sister," he said in his much deeper voice. "You are absolutely gorgeous!"

A tear ran down my cheek, and he wiped it away.

"There, there, Zura, I told you I would return someday."

"What took you so long?" I sniffed.

We hugged so hard I thought he would break me.

"I had to figure some stuff out and needed to make sure that when I entered your family again, that it was for the right reasons. Not because I was a scared little boy. Not because I was all alone, but because I knew this is where I could return with all the bad memories that haunted me these many years."

"Are you done, then?"

"Done?"

"Yes. Done figuring out that this is where you belong, Brother?"

He laughed a deep rich laugh. "Yes, I am done. I must say, Zura, you have grown." Tim looked me up and down. "No skinned-up knees, no bandages or cuts. You let your hair grow," he said. "I like it long." He tugged at my ponytail.

"Tim it's been so long."

"Not really. I've been secretly funding the sanctuary every year since I left."

"But why?"

"Because I wanted to make sure my family would be here whenever I decided to go home. So, I got an education, and here I am. The prodigal son has returned."

"Just like that?" I asked.

"Just like that. I had been communicating with Father for a month when I made up my mind what I was going to do," he said glancing at the woman by his side. "You should know, I never forgot you and wanted to come home sooner."

"But why? Since it's been so long since I've heard from you. I thought you had forgotten all about me."

"To be honest, at first, when I was young, I wanted to forget. I wanted to forget everything that we went through. And I tried. But I couldn't do it. I just couldn't forget about you. I did it for all of us. But, mostly for you, Little Sister."

His words made me cry and he dried my eyes with a white linen handkerchief that he pulled out of his pocket, as the man in the corner cleared his throat. It was the first time I cared that anyone else was in the room.

I pulled away to assess the visitors that traveled with Tim.

The man and the woman had the same broad smile and deep hazel eyes. I could tell that they were related by their features. Brother and sister, I guessed. They looked too much alike to be cousins.

The gentleman was slightly shorter than Tim. He had a kind, beautiful grin that showed dimples on his cheeks.

Our eyes connected for too long. As if neither one of us could look away. His smile was the most gorgeous smile I had ever seen.

Beside the man was a woman with short, curly blonde hair. She wasn't overly beautiful, but there was something magical in her eyes when she looked at me. Her smile mirrored that of the gentleman's smile, dimples and all.

Tim looked embarrassed that he also forgot about the others in the room.

"Sorry, where are my manners," he said. "Zura, this is Matthew Jones and Isabella. Matthew and I are friends from the university and, well, Izzy is Matt's sister and…my lovely wife."

I choked on the remaining cornbread crumbs in my mouth. I coughed and had to take a moment to swallow some tea before I could make sure that I heard Tim correctly.

"Izzy is your wife?"

"Yes, she is my wife," Tim said, taking her hand in his and kissing it tenderly.

Izzy smiled up at Tim with love and adoration that was impossible to miss.

The room went silent and everyone stared at me, seemingly waiting for my reaction. My parents shared a nervous look between them and back to Tim.

I wasn't sure why everyone was acting so curious about the news. Granted, having Tim just walk in and state that he was home, bringing two strangers with him, one being his wife, was a lot to swallow at one time. But that was Tim and me. We met in chaos, we survived in tragedy, and we united in an instant.

Maybe everyone thought that my feelings for Tim ran deeper than that of a brother and sister, nothing could be further from the truth. I loved him as a brother. That bond would forever be unbroken. No matter the distance, no matter the time, no matter the difference in the blood that ran through our veins, he was my beloved brother.

I grinned and reached for Isabella's hand, and she smiled.

"So, what size shoes do you wear?" I asked.

"I beg your pardon?" Isabella looked nervously back to Tim.

"Shoes. What size? That's what sisters do, isn't it? Borrow each other's things? Try on each other's clothes and shoes?"

Isabella relaxed. "Well, yes, I suppose that's what sisters do, though I only have my brother."

"So?"

"So?" she questioned.

"What size? I am dying to try on those heels!" I laughed and turned my attention to Tim. "You brought me a sister? Oh, Tim thank you!" I said wrapping my arms around Isabella. "That is truly the best birthday present that I could ever ask for, honestly. No offense, Tim, but sisters share a special bond," I winked at Isabella, and she giggled.

"It's nice to meet you, Zura. But I already feel as though I know you, the way Tim has always spoken of you. To be honest, I was a little jealous of you. I could not imagine anyone loving me as much as Tim loves you."

Tim stood beside his wife and held her hand.

"My darling, it's true that I love my sister, but I am sure that she is alright with how much I love you."

Momma moved to stand next to me and pulled Isabella into a motherly hug.

"Welcome to the family, Izzy."

"Thank you," Isabella blushed.

"Come on in everyone, I made plenty," Momma said.

Matthew stepped forward and shook my hand and smiled.

"It's very nice to meet you," he said with a gorgeous smile.

I wasn't used to feeling those butterflies in my stomach that he caused when he took my hand.

"It is nice to meet you too, Matthew."

"Just call me Matt."

"Alright," I answered, aware of my disheveled appearance. "It's nice to meet you, Matt."

He held my hand a little too long, and I couldn't seem to stop looking into those stunning brown and green eyes and his long lashes.

Momma interrupted.

"Alright, let's have a seat. Peter, please find a few more chairs." She beamed at me and I could feel the heat rising to my cheeks.

Momma served her porridge in a large silver bowl and placed the squares of cornbread on her beautiful flower plate in the center of the table. Tim sat beside me and dipped his bread into the mess that I made with the honey.

"We should just pass Zura's plate around There's plenty of honey right here," he teased, and I kicked him under the table. Tim laughed and rested a hand on my shoulder.

"How's the shoulder?" he said, and I stared at him in disbelief. My parents and I never talked about it. Tim cleared his throat, removed his hand from my shoulder, and changed the subject.

"I have more news, Zura," Tim said.

"I am not sure if my nerves can handle any more news today," I laughed, making eye contact with Matt, who sat across from me. His stare was unnerving.

Tim was beaming as he looked at his wife. "Zura, Izzy and I are excited to announce that we are going to be parents. You are going to be an aunt. Izzy is four months pregnant, and we decided that our child will be raised around family."

Momma jumped from her seat and crossed the room to hug the expecting Isabella.

"What wonderful news, right Zura?"

"I didn't quite know what to say. It was all happening so fast. Bringing a child into this world, into the African jungle, took me by surprise."

"Excuse me," I said, as I rose and walked out the screen door. I had a sudden urge to think and be alone. There was too much information, and I needed to take it all in and process it. So, I began to run. I ran from all of it and everyone. I ran through the field. I ran to the waterfall, and I climbed to the top of Thinking Rock. I amazed myself that I still knew which path would get me to the top the quickest.

I couldn't put a finger on what I was feeling. I felt happiness and sadness all wrapped up in a boiling pot of emotions.

I looked out at the rising sun. It wasn't directly overhead, not yet mid-morning. I heard him before I saw him. Fully expecting to see Tim, I was shocked when Matt appeared next to the waterfall.

"Zura!" he called out.

I swore under my breath. Clearly, Matt didn't understand the jungle and why you never yell or draw attention to yourself.

I climbed down before he got himself killed.

"Quiet, you fool," I said.

"Fool, is it? You just met me. It's a little too soon to determine that I am a fool, don't you think?"

"If you knew anything about animals, you would know that drawing attention to yourself would be very dangerous." I stood with my hands on my hips.

"You are probably right."

"Probably? Clearly you don't know that I grew up in this jungle, Mr. Jones. If anyone knows danger in the jungle, it's me." My shackles were raised.

Matt shoved his hands into his linen pants pockets.

"Tim is my best friend, and I know all about you, Jungle Girl. I have been fascinated by you for a long time. Ever since Tim and I met, and he told me what the two of you went through. I have wanted to meet you."

"Why?" I asked.

"Why? Because, as a child, you had so much passion for the jungle and the elephants. I have never seen that from grown-ups in America. I have been fascinated by Africa, and I wanted to do an internship here under your father's direction. Tim does as well. We will work side by side. I am also fascinated by the jungle girl who looks incredible in those tan shorts," Matt smiled at me.

"I see," I answered. Feeling exposed, I gave the bottom of my shorts a tug.

"You do?" Matt questioned. "So what do I have to do to get you to talk with me?"

"Talk with you?"

"Yes, about your life and this jungle."

I looked skyward and tapped my finger to my lips, just like I always did when I was contemplating something.

"I'll tell you what. Race me to the top of this big rock. If you beat me to the top, I will talk with you."

"And if I lose?"

"Then you do the dishes for a month."

"Deal," Matt stuck his hand out and I shook it. "On the count of three. One," he said and took off running.

I never saw anything like it. Matt scaled the side of the cliff with ease.

I ran after him and went to my favorite spot of Thinking Rock. The easiest path was my pick. Matt knew nothing if he couldn't see that path was easier just a few feet from where he started.

We both climbed close to each other like our lives depended on it. Hands and feet moved in unison. It felt so good to have a good reason to race to the top. I was about to pass Matt. I touched his shoulder. "You are about to lose," I bragged.

"And you are gorgeous when you climb."

We locked eyes and I lost my footing when it slipped off the rock. Matt grabbed my arm to steady me. I found my footing again, but not before losing any lead I thought I had.

As I hoisted myself up to the top, there he stood proud of his accomplishment.

"I win," he said, raising his hands over his head.

"You cheated!"

"I had to," he said spinning me around to face him. "I would much rather talk than wash your dishes."

"How did you learn how to climb so fast?"

Matt laughed deeply. "Do you think the jungle is the only place in the world that has cliffs? I have been climbing cliffs in Arizona ever since I can remember. Guess that makes us a match made in heaven."

"You wish. If you hadn't cheated, I would have had you. The next test will be how well you can swing from tree to tree."

"Well, where I grew up, there were not a lot of trees, so I am afraid you will have to teach me."

"Fine, but you are drying the dishes," I teased and began to climb down.

We stopped at the waterfall for a moment. "Do you want to see something?" I questioned.

"Lead the way."

I led the way up the side of the waterfall and into the mouth of the cave.

"Wow! This is a cool one!" Matt exclaimed. "There is one in Sedona that has actual paintings on its walls. Old and beautiful works of art."

"Who created the paintings?" I was fascinated to learn about the paintings and their origins in the United States.

"I am not sure. The drawings are interesting, and I like to find them and imagine their meanings, but I've never studied them."

"We also have other cave drawings here in Africa. Maybe we can take a trip and visit some of the sights."

"I'd like that a lot."

"Alright, let's make a plan to do that."

"It's a date. A rock climbing, cave exploring date. How could I have expected anything else from spending time with you? I can't wait." Matt smiled.

"It's not a date. Just an adventure. We will ask Father for his truck sometime soon and explore. I know several caves where we can find some drawings."

"Sounds like a date to me," Matt smiled.

We walked back to the house and bonded over the most fascinating cave drawing we have ever seen. It was great to have another person who wanted to explore and who seemed to enjoy the outdoors as much as I did.

That evening, after I finished my punishment from losing the bet, and Matt dried the last dish, I put away the last of the dishes and made myself some tea.

Momma and Father were sitting in our modest living room with Tim and Isabella. They discussed the house that they would build. The plan was to build on the hill behind our home. Not too close, but not too far away.

Isabella and Momma were talking about painting the walls in the kitchen, a bright sun-colored yellow to brighten up the space. They spoke of making curtains and how many bedrooms Isabella would want for their growing family.

It was too much for me. I was never one for planning spaces and sewing curtains, so I took my tea and went outside. I sat on the top porch step, carefully sipping my hot tea and watched the sun as it just met the top of the trees. It would be dark in an hour, and the jungle was coming alive with the sounds of predators getting ready for their feast.

Matt stepped out of the screen door.

"May I join you?" he said hesitantly.

"Of course," I said, sipping my tea and looking out at the setting sun.

Matt sat down beside me on the top step.

"Beautiful," he said.

I looked over at Matt. He wasn't looking at the horizon. He was looking at me.

It made me embarrassed and I looked into my teacup.

"You don't take compliments very well." Matt nudged me with his arm.

"The place isn't exactly crawling with suitors," I said, and we both laughed. "I have never been a fan of counting on people, especially men. I am independent by choice."

"Can you tell me more about you, Zura? I would like to hear it from your perspective."

"What do you mean by my perspective?"

"Tim has shared your story with me, mainly because we shared a room at school, and he would wake from horrible nightmares. Tim would tell me bits and pieces, and it took a long time for him to get the whole story out."

"Yeah, the nightmares are the worst part. It is not something that is easy to share. I guess you had to be there," I said jokingly. "What do you want to know?"

"Tell me about your life and your thoughts about your past."

"Well, that's a lot of information. I'm not sure we have that much time."

"Tell me your story and why they called you Jane. I have all the time in the world," Matt smiled, and those dimples on his cheeks drew me in.

"Okay. My story starts and ends in the jungle. I cannot think of a better place to have grown up, and there was a time when I hoped that I would live long enough to grow old. When I look back on that time in my life, I cannot help but feel powerful, yet weak, loved and hated, and proud but ashamed."

"Ashamed? Why ashamed?"

"I wanted those men to die. That's all I could focus on, watching them die so that I could live. Tim was the good that came out of the bad. How we met is a tragic story filled with pain and circumstances. How we came out of it alive is nothing short of a miracle."

"That's what Tim says as well."

"Yes. We had to rely on each other. It gave us a bond that few strangers could ever comprehend. Instantly, we were working as one mind and one being. We did what we had to do to stay alive, and we watched others die so that we could live. I am not proud of my part in it all, not really. But sometimes nature has a way of weeding out the bad so that the good can survive."

"You did what you had to do to survive," Matt said.

"Then there was Momma. I was worried sick about her fate. She was shot by Tim's uncle, and I didn't know if she was dead or alive. Let me ask you something. Have you ever loved someone so much that you could hear them in your mind, even when you were apart? You love them so much that their pain becomes your pain? When their happiness becomes your happiness? And when the thought of their death leads you toward the brink of insanity?"

"I can't say that I have."

"I have. But many years have come and gone, and time has the power to heal the pain of even the greatest losses. Time can numb the aching and memories fade away."

"You have such a passion, Zura."

"I owe that to my parents. They drilled lessons into my brain when I was young. They had to. I was a wild child. But time passes. Time is our enemy, it works against us, seemingly moving extremely slow when we look for it to pass quickly. It doesn't. It can't. It is one true constant in this world."

Matt nodded his head in agreement.

"Every day has twenty-four hours, and every week has seven days. You sound and think like a scientist. Interesting."

"I have spent my life surrounded by them. They come, but never really stay. There was one gentleman that studied time and the stars. He told me that it is always a matter of intensities. The bigger something impacts you, the more of that period you will remember. One slip, one fall from great heights can change your life forever. I have one of those memories. It is so vivid in my dreams, in my daily life, that it feels like it was only yesterday."

"Do you think you will ever get past it?"

"It's about perspective," I said, "Ten years is a long time, and I am a woman now. I live in a home some would consider paradise and others, a sort of hell. It's magical and scary all at the same time. I could not imagine ever leaving this place, for the jungle has always been my home. It is a part of me, so I will never leave it. No, I suppose I will never get past it. It's a part of me. But it has made me more cautious and yet stronger."

"You are very brave, Zura."

"I consider myself a survivor, not necessarily brave. When something bad happens, I always ask myself one question. *Is this the worst thing that has ever happened?* If the answer to that question is it's not worse than that time, I am in a good place. Some things are hard to explain, no matter how hard you try. Some wounds go deep, way down into your soul. And they change you. They make you grow up, or they make you grow old. But they become a part of you and your future self."

"I am excited to learn more about you," Matt said.

"Why are you so fascinated with my story?" I placed my empty cup on the porch beside me.

"Because your story is far more interesting than mine. You are also a beautiful, strong woman. Because you are fascinating, and because it looks as though we will be spending a lot of time together. How did you keep from reliving that time? How did you get past it? It took Tim a long time."

"Sometimes, my mind wanders, and it takes me back. Always in my dreams. I am not a good sleeper. It's usually times of high stress or sorrow. Those are usually the days where I am reminded just how far I have come, and I am proud of the woman I have become. You know, I can honestly say that racing you to the top of Thinking Rock today was the first time I was able to enjoy it for about ten years. Thank you. Thank you for giving me a memory that makes me smile when I think of it. By the way, you gloat way too much." I found myself giggling when I said it.

"I don't gloat," he said and brushed a loose tendril behind my ear. "You have such a beautiful smile."

The sentimental type, I thought.

"You most certainly do gloat. I wish you could have seen yourself. Arms raised above your head and grinning like a hyena."

"Hyenas grin?" Matt asked.

"Sure, they do. Hyenas also make a sound that sounds like a weird laugh."

"Fascinating. I can't wait to see and hear *that*."

"Careful, they like to follow lions to try to get a free meal."

"Good to know," Matt said. "You know your stuff, don't you?"

"If you are going to live in the jungle, you have to know what the dangers are, how to avoid them if you can, and how to get out of the way if you can't."

"I'll remember that," he said and leaned in.

"Hey, hands off my sister!" Tim laughed from the other side of the screen door. "You want me to take this guy out back and teach him some manners, Zura?" Tim came out of the door and stood casually on the porch.

I smiled at the two of them. Matt put his fists up like he was going to fight Tim.

"You can try, but I am afraid that I am completely innocent in this."

I slapped at his arm.

"Innocent! You are anything but innocent."

Tim laughed.

"You better watch her, Matt. Messing with Zura is like tangling with a lioness."

"He doesn't know me, Tim. He will find out." My joke died in the brownish smoldering eyes that stared into my soul.

"My dear, I feel like I have known you for a lifetime. It is not my fault that you have bewitched me. That's why I am innocent."

We shared an intense look that felt like it went on forever. That is, until Tim cleared his throat.

"Alright, I guess I will go back to house planning. I can see that my services are no longer needed or wanted here."

I felt embarrassed and put a little distance between us on the steps. I heard Tim speaking loudly to my parents and Isabella when he shut the screen door.

"Yeah, she's alright. In fact, I would say she is better than alright. Now, where were we?" Tim asked.

"The kitchen," Isabella announced.

"Of course, my dear. The kitchen, and the color of the sun on the walls, right?"

I giggled when I heard Tim. He clearly loved Isabella and there was no doubt that she loved Tim.

"That smile looks good on you," Matt said.

I tucked my hair behind my ear, unable to think of anything to say. Matt noticed everything. He was intense. He was also funny, witty, and smart. It was that smile that I found the most pleasurable. His kind and gentle hazel-brown eyes were alluring.

"Chocolate," I said, still thinking about his eyes.

"Chocolate? I compliment your smile, and all you say is chocolate? Where did you go just then? You looked like you were deep in thought."

I felt the blush creep like a vine up my neck and face. I had zero experience with men and had no idea how to tell him subtly that I was thinking about his eyes. So, I made up the first thing that came to my mind. "It's my birthday, so I was craving chocolate."

"Just like that? Out of the blue?"

"Yep. Chocolate is usually in every woman's mind, I guess."

Mathew's laugh came rich and deep.

"Zura, you are such an interesting woman. I can't wait to get to know you. You create a buzz in your family. You are the center of their world. I see it in everyone who loves you. Your parents are proud, your brother is proud, and it should give people hope that when they face hardship, that they can face it and rise above it. You are a strong woman, anyone could see it. And you survived a tragedy that most people would never be able to survive."

"It is true that I survived, but the dreams will always haunt me. In the pitch black, I relive the terror and the lives lost. Trauma does that to a person, especially when they are so young when the tragedy strikes. It grabs your spirit and takes hold, forever biting away at you to see whether you will crack, or are strong enough to endure."

"You do endure. You keep going," Matt said.

"I have to. It's not in my nature to crumble. Never have I been in another circumstance like the one that changed my family and me forever. They used to look at me as if at any moment, I would crack. I was afraid to put any more pressure on them. Especially my mother. She would always tell me that one day, I would be the cause of her having a heart attack. I was young and thought that her heart was somehow weak. I didn't want to be the cause of one more death. Especially my mother."

"That's a lot of pressure for someone so young to carry around."

"Well, it was her way when I was young, to try to keep me from doing dangerous things. I didn't listen anyway. I had such a need to be in the jungle and climbing, that I raced to the trees every moment I could."

"So, that experience prepared you for..." Matt struggled with finding the right words.

"Being kidnapped? Held against my will? Tied like a wild animal? Beaten, bruised and bloodied? Yep. That's only part of it. I had to rely on my instincts. Those few days of my youth taught me a valuable lesson. Be fearless, no matter what you must face. Be fearless. And resourceful. Stay on your toes and don't let your emotions guide your steps. Just plant your feet and move forward, no matter what happens."

"Is that what you plan to tell your children someday?"

"I'm not sure I will ever have children."

"Really, why not?" Matt asked.

"Well for one, this is a harsh world. If I did decide someday, my children would know the dangers and the joy of the jungle. I would be brutally honest with them so that I could prepare them for this world. The other reason is, this place isn't exactly overrun with eligible bachelors. I'm not going to marry the first monkey that comes along," I said with a laugh that broke the seriousness of our conversation. "Sure, there have been a few gentlemen that have wanted more than just to study the elephants," I laughed.

"Of course they did. Have you looked in a mirror, Zura? You are beautiful." Matt tucked my fallen hair behind my ear. "So, I have some competition?"

"Ha, ha," I was the only one that laughed that time. Matt stared deep into my eyes before he spoke. "Did you ever meet someone who changed your life forever?"

"Funny, I asked my Father that once."

"Really. And what was your father's answer?"

"He said twice."

"And what were those two occasions?"

"As I recall, he said the day he met my mother, and the day she gave him me," I smiled at the memory. "My bond to my Father is everything to me. He taught me everything I know. The animals and the way he loves his family are lessons that only he could have given me."

Matt smiled at me with those dimples, and I felt my heart skip a beat. I looked back at the door to see what everyone else was doing, and they were still engrossed in the house plans.

"Will you walk with me?" I asked Matt.

"Right now, I would walk off a cliff if you asked me to," he answered and grabbed my hand. Where do you want to go?"

"I want to show you a few things."

"Interesting," he teased.

We walked up the hill, and I showed him where we buried Chacha. I told him all about my loyal friend. We walked into the clearing, where Tembo usually stayed close to his family, even though, as a grown male, he was not in the herd anymore.

"Tembo, *nini!*" I called.

"What does that mean?"

"It's Swahili for come."

"So, your elephant speaks Swahili," he teased.

"I thought it was appropriate."

"I think you are right."

Tembo approached and eyed Matt with a low growl. He ruffled my hair with his trunk, just like he always did when he saw me.

Matt showed instant fear.

"Oh, he is so big up close. I'm not embarrassed to admit that I am a little frightened right now."

"Forget about his size."

"How could anyone forget? What happened to his ear?"

"An old injury. Close your eyes."

Matt closed his eyes and took a few deep breaths.

"Great, now put out your hand and reach out to touch Tembo."

"Matt's hand slowly rose. With hesitation, he gradually reached forward until his hand met Tembo's front leg."

A low vibration from Tembo caused Matt to pull away. He opened his eyes and he took a step backward in reaction to the growling.

"Maybe he doesn't like me being so close to the two of you."

"No, that's his happy sound. Astonishingly, he likes you. They say that elephants are a good judge of character."

"Really?"

"I don't know. I might have made that up. But I trust his opinion and he didn't try to trample you, so I would say that he likes you."

Tembo's trunk searched for Matt's head and he rubbed his hair. I was stunned and happy all at the same time.

Matt nudged me.

"What's with that look?"

"Oh, sorry. I am amazed that he is rubbing your hair."

Really, why is that? He did it to you."

"That's just it. He only does that to me. Nobody else. Not ever."

Matt caught the seriousness of the situation. "Ah, he does like me. That's wonderful! I guess I am welcome to stay."

"I guess you are."

Matt stood for a few minutes rubbing Tembo and touching his tusks.

"So, this is what all the fuss is about, Tembo. People kill your kind for this reason. Well, we will just have to stop them. What can we do? How can I help?" He rubbed Tembo's leg and trunk.

"Most people don't get the chance to get so close to the elephants."

"You mean the rest of the people; the scientists and veterinarians don't get close to him? Why, what's wrong with the others?" Matt asked.

"They keep their distance from Tembo unless it is to examine him. For that, they use me to keep him calm."

"Really, why?"

"Because he is wild animal, Matt. Because, as a male, Tembo isn't part of the herd anymore. But for some reason, he stays close to them. They all know what he did to Bain when he tried to kill me."

"Of course, he does."

"Does what?"

"Stays close."

Why, of course?" I asked stroking Tembo's trunk.

"If I were to guess, I would say he isn't exactly staying with the herd. He is staying because it keeps him close to you."

I found myself elated by his words.

"That is probably the nicest thing anyone has ever said to me."

"A blind man could tell that this animal loves you."

I felt myself getting emotional. A knot formed in my throat and I swallowed hard. "Yes, we were raised together. Tembo was orphaned, and my parents brought him to the sanctuary. We grew up together for a few years."

"Then how did he end up with the herd?"

"My mother reintroduced him to his herd, and they accepted him back. It was very hard for me. But we were reunited at the same time I met Tim. He rescued us."

"He rescued you?"

"Yes, he killed the man that was hunting me." I patted Tembo's leg. "Goodnight, my love,' I said to Tembo.

"Right, I remember Tim saying that he didn't see it because he was in a cave, but you told him how Tembo speared and crushed the man named Bain."

Matt and I walked and talked until the sun almost set. I was careful, as always, to make sure that we were back at the house before the night's carnage began. When we got back to the house, Tim and Isabella were sitting on the porch.

"Little Sister, I wondered where you took off to this time," Tim said, laying a protective hand on Isabella's stomach.

"I wanted to introduce Matt to Tembo."

"And how is our old friend?"

"He is wonderful. He has an older brother. He looks just like him. I call him Kendi."

"Amazing!" Tim said.

"Momma has known for years, but when I was young, I didn't really care too much about her work. Now, I could spend every day in the fields with her. You should take Izzy to meet Tembo tomorrow. Kendi does not let me ride him. Believe me, I've tried."

Isabella became excited. "Oh, I would love that."

I was embarrassed about my reaction to their exciting news, and I felt that I owed them an apology.

"Hey, look, I am so sorry that I walked out after you shared your baby news. I truly am happy for the both of you."

"We didn't mean to upset you," Isabella said.

I took her hand and patted it.

"You didn't upset me. I just had an emotional overload is all."

"I understand. I've had a lot of emotional overloads myself lately."

"So, have you picked out names?"

Tim became very excited to share the information with me. "We didn't exactly! If it is a boy, we are thinking of Peter, after Father. If it is a girl, we would like to call her Rose, after Momma. Maybe as her middle name. I like Kara as well."

"Kara Rose, excellent names. I love it. Did you tell Momma?"

"Yes. She cried." Tim beamed.

We all laughed.

"Looks like all the women are emotional right now," I said. "We all need some chocolate."

Tim stood. "I would like to have a moment with my sister if you don't mind," Tim said and bent down to kiss his wife's cheek. "We will be back in a few minutes."

Isabella smiled and looked at Matt.

"It looks like brother and sister time all around."

Matt sat beside Isabella and took her hand. "I am alright with that, Izzy."

Tim and I walked to the side of the house.

"Where is he?" Tim asked.

"Where is who?"

"Cha-cha, I didn't see him when we got here, so I assumed he was out hunting. How old is he now?"

"Come with me, I answered."

We walked up the hill behind the house. The grass was high from the recent rain storms, and the blades touched my bare legs as I walked.

Tim took my hand as we reached the crest. He looked down at the grave that I made for my dear beloved dog, and he wiped a lone tear away from his cheek.

"Tell me what happened to Cha-cha," he whispered.

"He got old. I noticed that he started to slow down, and one day he just crawled into my lap and passed away. I miss him terribly."

"I know you do, Zura. I know how much you loved him. He saved us more than once."

I nodded, unable to speak about our past. We kneeled beside Cha-cha's grave like I had done hundreds of times. I swallowed the lump that found its way to the back of my throat.

"Cha-cha missed you when you left. He searched for you for days. He was also your dog."

"No, Cha-cha had one true love, Zura, and that was you. He saved us because of you. That dog would have given his own life to save yours. He almost did."

"It's odd for me to talk about our past. Momma and Father never speak of it. It's too painful for Momma to remember that she almost lost me."

"Any parent would be devastated at losing their child. It's unnatural."

I pulled the weeds around Cha-cha's grave. "Still, I needed to talk it through and never could. I'm never having kids. I would make a terrible parent."

"You would make an excellent mother."

"No, I am too greedy with my time. I always told myself that I loved my time when my parents were not attentive. But now that I am older, well, I guess I see things differently."

How so?" Tim questioned and helped me pull the weeds.

"Well, for starters, had they been strict, I might not have been kidnapped and gone through that hell."

"True, I see your point. But Zura, had you been in that field with your mother, you could have been shot instead. And also, we would have never met."

I felt the need to change the subject.

"Let's head back. The sun is almost setting. I am sure Izzy wants to spend time with us." I looked down at the grave and kissed my palm. I placed it on the ground. "Goodbye, my loyal dog. I love you." I stood and faced Tim. "I need some therapy chocolate," I said sliding my arm into the crook of his.

"Therapy chocolate? What's that?"

"Oh, it's what women turn to when they are stressing about things. Chocolate makes the world a better place," I smiled and pushed Tim. He caught himself quickly.

"You better run, Sister. I am faster than I was as a kid," he teased as we both took off running toward the house.

The next day, I spent my time with Matt. I taught him how to feed the baby elephants and let him clean up the dung. It was a sort of initiation. I was amazed at how well he did. He didn't complain about any of the tasks that I gave him to do.

In the afternoon, he followed me to the field. I called for Tembo. I couldn't see him near the large herd, so I assumed he was by the water.

"Let's go down to the river and look for him. Sometimes he likes to hang out there."

Matt easily took my hand, and we walked about a half mile when Matt suddenly stopped. He turned me toward him.

"Zura." His eyes darted back and forth nervously.

"Matt, I want to see Tembo and then go back and have lunch with Momma,"

"Zura," Matt repeated. "I think we should go back. Let's go eat something now."

"Don't be silly…"

My words caught in my throat. They were strangled by the color of gray lying just beyond the trees. The disfigured ear from his youth gave away his identity.

"No," I whispered, and covered my mouth. My legs felt as if they would buckle. They could not hold my weight. I began to wobble like a new born animal taking its first steps.

Matt grabbed me and pulled me to him as he glided me to the ground. I pushed away from him and managed to find my footing as I stood on unstable legs. My screams came in sobs. I began to run toward the carnage.

"Tembo!" I cried, wilder than any wild animal.

All of my life, I have witnessed the devastation done by the poachers. I have helped to raise their offspring. But nothing could have prepared me for seeing my beloved friend taken down by man's greed.

When I reached Tembo's dead body, I sank to my knees beside his head. His tusks and trunk were taken.

I wailed with more violence than the strongest of storms, harder than any rushing waterfall. I threw myself across him, not caring that the flies had already begun to swarm.

Tembo's body was cool with death. His heartbeat was silent. Tembo was gone.

The devastation came as heavy as any thunderstorm, quick as the river, and as painful as a million stings.

My beloved friend lay on his side, his face mutilated by butchers. The very trunk that nestled my hair was gone. His wondrous tusks were stolen from him, and his eyes were set in a dead stare.

The vultures circled in the sky and several lions approached from the east, followed by the hyenas. The blood in the air of the freshly killed always enticed the hungry.

"We have to go, Zura," Matt whispered.

"No!" I screamed as he pulled me away from the slaughter. I didn't care about the approaching threats, I didn't care about anything. My tears spilled endlessly. Every wave brought on more grief, more anger. My heart was empty and broken into a million pieces.

Matt lifted me from Tembo and carried me away from the carnage. I was inconsolable. Grief boiled up inside of me, as wild as any threat. My screams could only be compared to the lion's roar. The ferocity went beyond any pain I had ever felt. With clenched fists I beat on Matt uncontrollably and he let me.

Matt carried me back to the house. The entire way, he tried without luck to soothe me. His voice was calm, and he held me close while I continued to beat on his back and his arms.

Momma came running out door when she heard me wailing in heartache.

"What has happened?"

Father and Tim came running from Father's office, and Isabella stood on the porch.

Matt placed me on the porch and Momma and Isabella encircled me with hugs and rubs and kisses.

"Zura, please," Momma pleaded. "Please do not cry like that, tell me what is wrong. Whatever it is, we will work through it together."

Matt stood next to the bottom step.

"It's Tembo. They got him."

I could hear Momma's cries softly next to my ear. Her body moved with each gasp. We cried with more violence than the winds of a hurricane, falling slowly together onto the porch. Momma's head pressed against mine in mutual wretchedness. She began to rock back and forth, taking me with her, in a soothing movement to calm our devastation.

Isabella rubbed my back and whispered.

"It's all right, Sister. You cry it out. We are all here for you."

After several minutes, I picked up my head from Momma's shoulder and looked at Tim. He shook his head, his eyes brimming with tears. "All the money in the world, and we still couldn't protect him." Tim knelt on the top step and hugged me from behind. "I know, Zura. I know. We probably wouldn't be alive today if it weren't for Tembo. We owe him our lives, and we couldn't protect his."

I looked at Matt.

"You said he stayed for me. He stayed to be close to me. I am the reason that he is dead."

Matt's head shook in denial.

"No, Zura. That's not what I meant. You gave Tembo all the love in the world. He knew it. I read once that elephants are very smart. Tembo knew you. He saw you as his family."

"What do you know?" My anger rose and spilled over like a pot of boiling water set on the fire too long. "You know nothing. You come to Africa with your education and knowledge from books. You have no idea about what an elephant is or how they feel!"

Matt became the target of my despair. I lashed at him like a hungry lion ready to make her kill.

Matt paced in front of me, afraid to speak. Afraid to aggravate me more. His hands were in his hair, his feet moved in a nervous pattern, back and forth he shuffled. Matt looked as though he wanted to walk away before I could continue to dig. But I did; I dug and dug until his emotions gave way to a shallow grave. His head dropped in defeat. He had the sense to know that he could never win the battle against a distraught female.

Tim held me tighter.

"This is in no way your fault. You did not create this, just as you could not have prevented this." Tim stroked my hair.

There was only one place that I knew I would find the comfort I needed. I rose and walked to my father. He was my constant, my rock. Father opened his arms wide and I fell into them. He cradled me just as he did when I was a child. He hushed the reality that swirled in my mind. Father let me cry and spoke softly in my ear.

"You were the light in his darkness, you were his sun. He was yours, completely devoted to you. Please do not shut out all the good memories. He wouldn't want it that way."

The tragedy made me doubt, it made me question if all of the hard work we put into Wild Hearts was making a difference. We were such small creatures in a great big jungle. What difference could we possibly make?

My Tembo was gone, shot near our home, his home. Butchered, mutilated for the tusks that protected me, that killed Bain. A boundless emotional flood unleashed that went deeper than sorrow. It was too much for me to bear any longer. Years of burying the grief and horror of my childhood and now the loss of Tembo rushed like the waterfall and spilled into my soul.

CHAPTER 14

I lost track of the days. Was it a week? A month? One day melted into the next. How many sunrises did I miss? How many starry skies had passed?

I just laid in my bed, sick from the grief that controlled my entire body.

Momma and Isabella were constantly in my room, trying to cheer me up. They talked about curtains and making blankets for the baby. Momma rubbed my feet to try to soothe me. Nothing worked. I was numb. My soul was broken, dying from a loss that never should have happened the way it did.

The knock on my door was light, but the voice rich and deep. "Zura, it's Matt. May I come in?"

"You have been coming in here every day. I've never stopped you." I wiped at my face and tried to brush my hair with my fingers, knowing that there would be no fixing my disheveled appearance and tear-stained cheeks. My hair had not seen a brush in days.

There was no sign from the other side of the door, but I knew he was there.

"You can come in, Matt."

The door opened slowly and he stood in the doorway, holding flowering wild verbena.

"I thought these might help."

I stared at him for a moment. No one had ever presented me with flowers.

"Thank you. They do help with heartburn, but I am afraid not a broken heart. It was very kind of you."

Matt walked over and set the flowers on my window sill. He turned with confidence.

"Can I ask you a question, Zura?" He stood at the bottom of my bed.

"Alright," I answered. I sat up straighter.

"Do you think this is what Tembo would want for you?"

I felt my shackles go up.

"What do you mean?" I asked.

Matt cautiously walked to me and sat on the bed.

"Do you think Tembo would be happy to know that you want to rot in your room for the rest of your life, unable to function?"

I thought for a moment and could tell in what direction our talk was going.

"No, I suspect Tembo wouldn't."

"So, what are you going to do about it?"

"What can I do about it? I can't bring him back."

"Use the energy and emotions to steer you forward. Make Tembo's death a reminder of the travesties that still exist in this world. Stand up for the rest of the elephants. Create an organization of awareness."

"If we can't protect them here, then what good is an organization? You are in Africa's jungle now. Not in a board room, not in the United States where laws and changes are made easily."

"Trust me, spending time in any big city in the United States is also a jungle. It's just a different kind. You are in a unique situation to make a difference. The people in the United States will listen. The men with all of the money and fame will see the benefit of helping if there is something in it for them. That's where you need to get your story out."

"Yes, I can see what you mean. But, I am just one person. What difference can I make?"

"Are you or are you not the same person that survived in a jungle with those very dangerous men? Where is that little girl whose fight and spirit made her a survivor?"

"She's still here somewhere."

"Well, find her. Pull her out. We need her."

"We?"

"Yes, everyone is sick from worrying about you. Show them how much you loved Tembo. Put that love for him into your work. You can pick yourself up and make his life mean something. Look at all the good that happens here. Look at how many lives have been saved. Start an organization to get the word out. Create an awareness of what travesties are happening here."

I sat up.

"So where would I start?"

Matt smiled.

"Start by getting out of this bed. Start with your family. Tim will financially support your cause; you know that. Izzy is a natural organizer and planner. She is dying to feel useful here. Give her a job. Work with her. It will help take her mind off how fat she is getting," Matt teased as he took my hand.

I slapped his arm. "She's not fat! She's pregnant," I laughed for the first time in days and it felt good.

Matt's hearty laugh matched the beauty of his grin.

"I'm her brother. If I didn't tease her, she would think something was wrong. We can't have that, can we?" Matt kissed the back of my hand.

"No we can't have that," I answered.

"So, what's it going to be, Jungle Girl? Are you getting out of that bed or do I have to drag you out?"

"Okay, okay. I really appreciate the talk, Mr. Jones. Can I see the flowers?"

Matt rushed over to the window and returned holding the bouquet.

I breathed in their sweet smell. They smelled of the outdoors and sunshine. I realized how much I missed both.

Matt's face lit up.

"I got it! We can call it the Tembo Project!"

"That's a strong idea. It literally means Elephant Project. Nicely done, kind sir," I said.

Matt placed his hand on my shoulder and rubbed it gently.

"There it is."

"There what is?" I questioned.

"That gorgeous smile." Matt ran his thumb over my lips and cupped my face.

I could feel the blush paint my cheeks. "Let's go tell Izzy that we need her help."

"Yes, my sister is an angel and would do anything for anyone. You, my dear, I am afraid, you are not an angel," Matt said.

"I'm not? Why not?"

"There is an evil in you," he said and kissed my hand again.

"Matthew Jones, there most certainly is not evil in me. But I am very sorry for the way I lashed out at you the other day. Please forgive me."

"Alright, then you're a witch!" Matt brushed off my apology and tried to tickle me.

"I am no witch!"

"You most certainly are a witch. You have put a spell on me. You have bewitched my heart from the moment I met you."

I felt the heat continue to rise from my neck to my cheeks.

"Alright, maybe I am a witch then. And what do you intend to do about it?" I asked, placing my hands on my hips.

Matt tapped his finger on his lips. I had to smile at the motion that mirrored my action when I am pondering something. Matt raised his finger from his lips and lifted it into the air.

"I am afraid there is only one way to break the spell," Matt said as he tucked my hair behind my ear. "I will have to make you my wife. Then you will have to obey me. You will have to do what I say and remove the spell."

"Don't you think that's a little extreme? Maybe I would like to keep the spell on you," I said laughing.

Matt's face became serious. He pulled me toward him, and I wrapped my arms around his neck.

"No, I do not think it's extreme."

"I really don't think I am the obeying type." I whispered, my mouth suddenly dry.

"I think it will be the best idea that I've ever had. Marry me, Zura. Let's grow this family, right here with everyone that you love. You are surely a risk taker. Take a risk with me. Let's get married, what do you say?" Matt babbled on too much.

"I say that it's way too early in our relationship for you to be asking me such a serious question."

"It's not too early. I've come to know you over the last few weeks. We are a match."

"I am a woman who has never needed a man for protection, for guidance, or for someone that I must obey." I looked away to fiddle with the sheet on my bed.

Matt placed his fingers under my chin and moved my face to his. Our eyes locked in the seriousness of the conversation.

"No," I answered.

"No?" he questioned. "You must know that we belong together, Zura. You are the woman for me."

"I don't want to be a wife, to be a mother. Not here. Not when I could lose a husband or a child to the dangers that can lurk right outside our door."

"I will protect you, protect our children." Matt's eyes did not waiver.

I laughed at his answer. "How would you protect me? I am the one who knows this jungle. I have lived in it my whole life. It is me who would have to protect you."

"Marry me," Matt said, pulling me close.

"No," I answered. "I can't marry you. I can't become a mother. The risk is too great."

"Your parents didn't think so. They gladly had you and you are their whole world. Your Father speaks of nothing else. He loves you with all of his heart. So does your mother."

I pondered his words before I answered. "Yep, they do. But look what happened. I was in danger."

"Not by the jungle. That was the men's doing." He answered. "That's the real problem, isn't it? That time in the jungle. Will you ever put it behind you? Will you always give them the power to hurt you?"

"Yes. No, I mean. They have no power. They are dead. I know because I helped to kill them."

Matt ever so slightly shook my shoulders.

"You didn't kill them, their greed killed them. Not you. Don't give them the power to control your life. Take your life back. Take a chance. I know you have feelings for me. Maybe even love me. Take a chance on me. I will never let anyone hurt you. I promise. Marry me. What do you say?"

"I say you talk too much," I said and kissed him.

"Is that your answer then?" Matt grinned.

"I guess it is. But if you decide to run off, know that there is nowhere in this blasted jungle that you can hide that I won't find you," I laughed. "I will marry you, Mr. Jones."

"I knew I could convince you."

"Wear me down is more like it."

Matt grabbed my hand and pulled me to my feet. The flowers scattered onto my bed and the floor. I reached to pick them up, but Matt tugged on my arm.

"Let's go tell the family. They have been worried sick. Your mother will stop pacing outside your door."

"Something will happen that will cause her to pace again, rest assured; that's my mother."

Day after day, I found joy in the blooming relationship with Matt. He was always so sure of his decision to ask me to marry him. Never a doubt about me, about my past, or about our future. Matt became my steadfast companion.

He worked beside Father daily, learning the veterinarian tips and tricks for dealing with the wild animals that lived at Wild Hearts.

The next spring was filled with new life. Isabella gave birth to a boy. They named him Peter Matthew Warren. My parents gushed over Little Peter every day. He had Tim's hazel eyes, but Izzy's blond curly hair. Little Peter was a tiny cherub with chubby little cheeks. He was the most adorable baby, and we loved him so much. He made me a little uncomfortable; I had never spent time around babies before, but I couldn't help but hold him close and rock him into slumber. As long as I reached him before Momma got her hands on him. If she reached him first, it was all over. She would always say that it was a *grandmother thing.*

***

Momma fussed with my hair, putting my crown of flowers in just perfectly over my long curls. She wore the same flowers in her hair.

"Zura, I never thought I would see the day that you would get married." Momma wiped a stray tear from her eye.

"Well, me either, to be honest. He all but begged me," I said as I looked at myself in my full-length mirror. "It was impossible not to fall in love with him." I couldn't stop giggling. I was so happy.

I wore a white lace dress, just like the one in my dreams as a child, I had my crown of flowers, and I was indeed the princess of the jungle.

Mother's flowing beige dress caught the air that blew through the window. "You couldn't have picked a better day for the wedding, sweetheart. There is not a cloud in the sky. The field is a perfect place to celebrate too. Maybe the elephants will attend."

"Maybe they will knock over the tables we set up last night. Have you seen Matt yet, Momma?"

"No, he was pacing with your father earlier, so I let them be. Your father was telling him that story of how he met me."

"I always love when he tells that story. Momma, I learned what love should look like from watching you and Father. The way he used to sweep you up into a dance and kiss you, I always hoped to find someone who loved me just as much."

"You did, I am sure of it. It's in Matt's eyes, every time he looks at you."

"That's true. Matt does love me. I knew just how much when Tembo died, and he encouraged me to start the Tembo Project. I will always be grateful for the way he encouraged me and continued to support me as I built the project. Do you think he will pass out when he sees me in a dress? He's never seen me in anything but shorts."

Momma laughed.

"I think we will be picking him up off the ground. That's what I think. You make the most beautiful bride, Zura." Momma wiped her happy tears with her handkerchief.

Isabella knocked on my door.

"It's just Little Peter and me. Can we come in, Zura? We didn't want to miss all the fun."

I opened the door for Isabella. She walked in with Little Peter, who was chewing on his fingers and dripping drool all over his chubby hand. "Is it too young for him to get teeth, Momma? He has been fussy and chewing and drooling all day long," Isabella said. "Oh, Zura! Look at you! You are stunning! Those pearl earrings look amazing with the dress."

"Thank you, Izzy. Thanks for letting me borrow them."

"Oh, you are welcome. That's what sisters do, right? Borrow each other's things?" Isabella winked at me and began to bounce a fussy Little Peter.

"You look amazing too. That pink and cream dress is stunning on you."

"Does it look too tight?" Isabella asked, pushing her short blonde curls from her eyes. I am starting to get my figure back after having Peter. Tim says he doesn't mind the extra curves. Men," she laughed. She held Little Peter out to Momma's waiting arms.

Momma continued the bouncing movement and added a sway, which I guessed came natural to mothers. She kissed Little Peter's head.

"There's my little jungle prince. How did you sleep last night?" she said.

"He didn't," Isabella said wiping the baby drool off the front of her dress.

"Welcome to motherhood," Momma announced. "There were weeks that I thought I'd go out of my mind over Zura. I swear she always wanted to give me a heart attack as a child."

"Oh, Momma, I haven't heard you say that in years," I laughed and kissed her cheek.

Father knocked and called through the door.

"Is everyone decent?"

"Come in, Peter," Momma called. Come look at our beautiful daughter." She wiped a tear, kissed my cheek, and carried Little Peter out of the room.

Isabella turned and hugged me.

"We will see you outside. I love you, my sister."

"I love you too. Oh, and Izzy?"

"Yes?" She turned around to look at me.

"Thanks for the shoes, dear sister," I said, raising my dress to let her see.

Isabella laughed and hugged me. "That's what sisters are for. I'll go calm down my brother. He is probably pacing profusely."

Momma and Isabella went outside and the screen door slammed behind them.

My father stood staring at me.

"You truly are a vision of beauty, Zura." He said and grabbed my hand to spin me around in a circle. "Just beautiful. You make me proud, Zura. Not just because you are my daughter, but because of the woman you have become."

"Thanks, Father."

"No, I mean it. You always take a tragedy and find a way to make it better in the end. I know we never talk about it because it upsets your mother. But like when you were young, and you were in the jungle with those men, you brought home Tim. You made something tragic into something beautiful. You gave us a son, who now has given us another daughter and our first grandchild. We are hoping for many more, by the way."

"Oh, Father, please. Can I at least have my wedding first?"

"And the day that you brought Cha-cha home. You wouldn't take no for an answer, and he turned out to be your fierce protector until the day he died."

"Yes, I miss Cha-cha. He was so unique and wild, yet loyal. Like we were his pack."

Father hung his head a little.

"And of course, Tembo."

"Oh, how I wish he could be here today. I wish I could have ridden into the field on his back. I miss him every day."

"I know you do. I do too."

We heard the screen door slam and hurried footsteps coming down the hall. "Little Sister, can I come in?"

"Of course, you can come in, Tim! I can't believe you stayed away this long! Where have you been?"

"I was getting your chariot, my lady," Tim bowed and offered his arm to me, and I wrapped my arm around his."

"Well then, let's not wait another moment, my good man. Shall we go?"

"After you," he bowed.

Father placed his hand on my shoulder.

"I am afraid that I will be unable to walk with you." He kissed my head. "I love you, and I will see you at the wedding." With that, he turned and left the house.

I stood there shocked and looked at Tim.

"Did I do something wrong?"

"No, you didn't do anything wrong."

"Well, did Matt upset Father in some way?"

"No, Matt is in the field, waiting for you."

"What is it then, are you walking me to the field?"

"Not exactly," Tim said sheepishly, grabbing my arm and pulling me out of the bedroom. "Just come with me."

Tim led me out on to the porch. I stood in disbelief when I saw him. He was brilliant; his long tusks were high, his trunk lifted toward the sky. Except for his ear, he looked just like his brother. Kendi stood tall, with a beautiful embroidered blanket on his back. The colors reminded me of the sun as it's just coming up over the trees. I reached out to touch it.

"It's the most beautiful thing I have ever seen."

"Izzy has been working on that for months."

"She made this for me?"

"She made it for you. She said it gave her a thrill to do something for her sister. So Little Sister, your chariot awaits. Give the command."

"Give the command?"

"Yes, he knows what to do."

"How? How does he know?"

"Matt and me. We taught him. And you thought we were lazy and not working."

Excitement grew inside of me.

"Kendi, *chini. Chini*, Kendi."

Kendi slowly lowered himself. Tim placed a small stool on the ground for me to climb up on Kendi's back.

"Normally, I would just climb up and be done with it. I'm not sure I could do it in a dress, but I would have tried."

Tim laughed. "Yes, I know. Matt thought of that, and that's why he has this stool for you to use. He said to please make sure that you get to the field before you get dirty."

"Ha ha, very funny."

Tim grabbed my arm and helped me to get on Kendi's back without incident. Kendi stood and let out a low groan that reminded me of Tembo.

"Oh, and here's one more finishing touch." He reached into a bag and pulled out a long garland of flowers. "Drape this over Kendi's neck. We can't have him improperly dressed for the wedding."

"Tim! This is beautiful!"

"Momma helped me. Okay, we're ready. He looked up at me and smiled. "You have changed my life, Zura. You gave me a family; you gave me a purpose. I love you, Little Sister."

"I love you too, Tim. Now let's go, or you will make me cry before we even get there." I was getting excited and nervous at the same time. "Let's go before the groom changes his mind."

"Yeah, we don't want him running off," Tim joked.

"Where would he run that I couldn't find and catch him?"

"So true, Little Sister, so true."

Tim led Kendi by a rope fashioned into a rein. When we reached the field by the house, I could see the work that went into erecting a white tent adorned in flowers that made a path to Matt.

Momma stood holding Little Peter and wiping her eyes. Next to Momma stood Isabella.

Father met us in the field and took the rein from Tim. He looked up at me proudly. Father led me the rest of the way. After we stopped, and I gave Kendi the command, he helped me off Kendi's back.

Father joined the family and placed a comforting arm around Momma. It was pleasing to see them, but as soon as I saw Matt in his white button-down shirt, his burgundy colored suspenders, and tan pants I smiled. He wore a tan fedora hat that made him look distinguished and very handsome.

Behind him, stood the herd. I am sure it must have been a coincidence, but it was fitting to have them close. So many standing tall and strong. Little ones were staying close to their mothers, unsure of the great big world.

The wedding ceremony was short, but we danced under the stars for hours. It was as if everyone else had disappeared when I looked at Matt and he held me in his arms. He became my world, and I, his.

"Who do you love?" he asked, kissing my forehead.

It was the same game we'd played a hundred times. "I love Momma and Father," I said, ignoring his kisses.

"Who else do you love?" He kissed my cheek.

"Oh, that's easy. I love Tim and Izzy and Little Peter."

"And who else do you love?" he said, and he kissed my lips.

"You. I love you." I whispered.

CHAPTER 15

June, 1936

As I sit with my daughter on my lap on the porch of our modest remote home, I remember the whispers of time that have passed. Somewhere, deep inside of me, that little girl still lives. She is very much alive. She wants to climb the jungle's trees and reach the tallest peaks. That little girl could conquer all that is wild and free in her life-force, unafraid of the vast wilderness, unafraid of what could be lurking in every corner of this great big world.

My sweet, four-year-old daughter, Olivia, looks up at me with those deep hazel eyes as I stroke the curls of her wispy chestnut hair. It is getting longer now, but still barely touches her tiny shoulders. Her light skin that tans as quickly as my own has a golden hue. Her little hands rest on my arm. She smells of earth and flowers and all things good and innocent.

Olivia has a high, soft voice when she speaks.

"Mommy, tell me a story."

"What story would you like to hear?" I question.

"My favorite one."

"You mean the silly story about the monkeys in the trees?" I tickle her belly until she laughs.

"No, not the monkeys," she giggles.

"What about the hippo that had a terrible toothache?"

"No, not the hippo. The one about Jane," she squeals with delight.

In truth, I already know her favorite story, for I have told that tale to her many times. And every time, she is just as enchanted with the story as though she had never heard it before.

"Please, Mommy, please! Tell me about Jane!" She begins to move excitedly on my lap. "Start like you always start. Tell it like you are Jane."

"Okay, my sweetheart, I will tell you the story, but you have to promise to eat all of your dinner tonight."

"Even the vegetables?" She flutters those long lashes, barely hiding the yellow, brown, and green of her scrutiny.

"Even the vegetables."

Olivia lets out a huge, dramatic sigh. As she thinks about my offer, she presses her little finger against her lips. With her eyes directed skyward she stalls, hoping I will change my mind. I am silent.

She gives me her prettiest smile. That grin never stops melting my heart. It's identical to her father's smile, that same smile I'd seen on his face the day we met. She is too young to know what power her smile holds, with those dimples on her cheeks.

"Deal!" Olivia squeals as she puts her hand out to shake mine.

I take her hand and bring it to my lips for a kiss.

"Deal," I answer.

She is quick with her grin and laughs as I tickle her bare feet.

"Stop! We gotta pinkie swear. Remember, Mommy?" Olivia sticks her little pinkie out, and I wrap mine around hers.

"How could I forget?"

I inhale and let out a deep breath before I allow myself to go back to that time and place. Time has made it somewhat easier to revisit those nightmares. Though, most of it is still so vivid, as if it only happened yesterday. I remind myself that it was long ago and that I am older and different than I was when I was facing those tragic few days. When I tell it as a story, I can detach myself from the events. I can pretend it is nothing more than an adventure.

I do not believe in sugar-coating anything for Olivia. Not here. Not when she is growing up in one of Africa's jungles. I always vowed to be honest with her, so that she is aware, even at a young age, of how life can be in this dangerous and wondrous world.

Although she still hears it as just another story, a fairy tale, someday she will know that this story is unlike the other stories. It is different than those I read to her from her books. This story is real. Real, because I am still alive to tell the tale. Real, because I have the scars as proof.

"Let's see, where should I start?" I position myself comfortably for the long story ahead.

Olivia jumps with excitement.

"Start with how wild she is. Tell me about the elephants, and Tim, and how sad she was about her mommy, and the bad men. Don't leave anything out. I want to be just like Jane when I get older. I want to climb and hunt and do all the things you say that I am too young to do."

"Olivia, you are only four. She was older than you when she could do those things."

"Didn't her Mommy get mad when she did all that stuff?"

"Yes, her Mommy got very upset with her."

"Okay, okay!" Olivia grew impatient as she usually did. "Tell me why they called her Jane."

"Alright," I began. "A long time ago and not so far away, there lived a girl named Zura, but they called her Jane."

Matt and Tim pulled up in the truck, sending a cloud of dust into the air. Olivia sat up excitedly, rubbing her eyes.

"Daddy! Uncle Tim! Where is Grandpa?"

"Hello, my sweet girls," Matt said from the passenger seat. "Grandpa is taking care of a monkey with a belly ache, Olivia."

"Can I go and watch? Please? Grandpa said I could go and help when I am older. Today, I am older than yesterday," Olivia reasoned.

I laughed and hugged her tight. "You have not had lunch young lady, and then it is nap time for you. After a nap, Granna wants to bake with you."

"Oh, I can't skip the baking. Granna won't know what to do without me. Daddy, Mommy is telling me the story. Do you want to hear it?"

"Sure, I do," Matt said as he joined us on the porch. He gave us both a kiss, and he smiled down at my protruding belly and gave it a rub. "Looks like you are carrying a boy, that's what Izzy said anyway. And she would know, she has three children."

"The twins are getting so big, aren't they? Olivia loves to play with them and hold them. When we were visiting the other day, Cora was rolling over and, Kara was most content just lying there and looking up at Olivia's face. Little Peter wants nothing to do with them. He said that girls are stupid, and he wanted a brother."

"Oh, I bet Izzy boxed his ears for that."

"She made him sit with his sisters and apologize. It became quite the show."

Olivia fidgeted on my lap. She called out to Tim.

"Uncle Tim, do you want to hear the story?"

"What story, baby?" Tim said unloading supplies from the back of the truck.

"Oh, it is my favorite story. It's the one about the girl in the jungle called Jane. You gotta hear how it ends, Uncle Tim. Just skip to the end, Mommy." Olivia crossed her little arms over her chest.

"No, Olivia, I think I know how that story ends," he said and gave her a wink.

Olivia turned her attention back to me. "Just tell me the end, Mommy." Olivia played with the silver elephant on her necklace. "Tell me what happens next to Jane."

"You know what happens next, silly girl," I said and tickled her feet again.

"Tell me, tell me! You gotta say it the way you always do."

"You *have to* say it," I corrected.

"Okay, you have to say it the way you always do," Olivia pleaded.

"Alright," I said and kissed the top of her head. "And they lived happily ever after."